Verses and Poems
& Stories to Tell

by Dorothy Harrer

*Dedicated to the children for whom they were made
in The Rudolf Steiner School, New York City*

Printed with support from the Waldorf Curriculum Fund

Published by:
Waldorf Publications at the
Research Institute for Waldorf Education
38 Main Street
Chatham, NY 12037

Title: *Verses and Poems & Stories to Tell*
Author: Dorothy Harrer
Editor: David Mitchell
Layout: Ann Erwin
Proofreader / Copy editor: Ann Erwin
Cover illustration from *Pico the Gnome* by Martina Müller,
   with permission of the artist

© 2014 by Waldorf Publications
Second edition
ISBN# 978-1-936367-58-0

Table of Contents

Verses and Poems

The First Graders	5
School Days	5
To Give Thanks	5
Numbers	6
From Big Voice to Tiny Voice	7
For Follow the Leader	7
My Kingdom	8
Dream Words	8
The Tree	8
The Seasons	9
God's Gifts	9
Poem for C.K.	10
Poem for J.B.	10
Poem for R.D.	11
Building Houses	11
The Number Four	13
Four Kinds of Sentences	14
The Four Elements	15
The Earthworms	15
Horses in the Rain	16
Mouse in the House	16
The Animals in Me	16
The Lion's Pride	17
The Wheat and the Bread	17
Verses for Children	18

The Fairytale Stories

The Prince Who Couldn't Read 19
The Secret and Magic Name of the King 25
The Princess of the Golden Stairs 30
The Soldier, the Huntsman and the Servant 36
Three Sisters 41
The Fir Tree (A Christmas Story) 46

The Nature Stories

The Lazy Gnome 50
The Lazy Water Fairy 54
The Four Seasons 57
The Rainbow 60
The Prince of Butterflies 64
The Snowflake 68

Other Stories

Four Words 70
The Boy and the Tree 71
The Stag, the Lion and the Eagle 73
The Four Brothers 76
The Story of a Child 79
A Time of War. 86

The First Graders

We've come to school
With faces clean
And hair well-combed
As you have seen.

Our shoe-strings tied,
And ribbons too,
We're here to learn
Just what to do.

To write, to read,
To count, to play,
To be good friends
In every way.

School Days

See how the earth gives us ground to stand on.
So what we do rightly makes us strong.

See how the flowers make us happy with their colors.
So our thoughts for others make us happy too.

See how the animals help to clothe and feed us.
So our help to others will teach us to be wise.

See how each day we may learn our lessons
That we may become happy, strong and wise.

To Give Thanks

I thank the earth beneath me
For there I stand and walk.
I thank the air around me
Which helps me breathe and talk.

I thank the sun so warm and bright.
I thank the stars who shine all night
So far away in Heaven's height
To keep me safe till morning light.

Numbers

When at first we look for 1
We find it in the shining sun.

For me and you
We count 1, 2.
The day, the night,
The dark and light,
The good, the bad,
The gay and sad,
The girl, the boy
We count with joy.
They all are 2s
Which we can use.

Father, mother and child we see
And count them quickly: 1, 2, 3.

That we have 4 seasons we know very well,
As well as 4 elements with which we dwell.
And 4 kingdoms of nature to you we can tell.

The number of fingers I have on one hand
Are 1, 2, 3, 4, 5.
Five toes on each foot help me balance and stand.

Whoever counts his fingers knows
He has the same amount of toes.
1, 2, 3, 4, 5, 6, 7, 8, 9, 10.

Eyes, ears, hands, and feet!
4 pairs has everyone we meet.

We count the hours of the day
And when we do we always say:
1, 2, 3, 4, 5, 6, 7, 8, 9, 10, 11, 12.
We count the months in every year
And when we do then you will hear,
1, 2, 3, 4, 5; 6, 7, 8, 9, 10, 11, 12.

The different numbers of the earth
Have been around us since our birth;
But no matter how hard we try
We cannot count all the stars in the sky.

From Big Voice to Tiny Voice

I am the giant.
When I mumble and grumble,
The whole earth doth rumble.

I am the gnome.
I dig in the ground
That gold may be found.

I am the witch,
And I spit, and I spat
With my skinny black cat.

I am the King.
I hold in my hand
The laws of the land.

I am the Knight.
I fight the King's foe
With battle-axe and bow.

I am the Queen
In my shining crown
And silvery gown.

I am the Lady.
I primp and I preen
And I follow the Queen.

I am the fairy.
I fly in the air
And live everywhere.

I am the elf.
I whisper and peep.
I hop, skip and leap.

For Follow the Leader

Fairies are flying,
Elves are skipping,
Dwarfs are dancing,
Giants are tramping,
Hunters are galloping,
Dragons are prancing,
And the children tip-toe to school.

My Kingdom

The rocks are sleeping on the ground,
The trees dream of the sky,
The beasts creep in the forest deep,
And a royal King am I.

My Kingdom reaches far and near,
My golden crown stands high,
I rule rocks, trees, and creeping beasts.
The King of all am I!

Dream Words

Far sails the sailor,
Green sweeps the sea,
While the wind blows over the yellow sand
And dragons are dancing in dragon land
To a musical tune
By the light of the moon
Who shines in a moon-horn tree.

The Tree

Under the great, green tree
There's shade for you and me.
And up where the green leaves give green shade
The robin's cozy nest is made,
Which none can see.

But in Autumn's breath so chill
And the creeping frost so still
Green leaves have turned to red and brown,
And one by one they've fallen down.
The birds have flown—
And the empty nest is there
On branches bare
For all to see.

The Seasons

Where did old King Winter go
With his robes of swirling snow,
His frosty crown and his icy spear,
And the North Wind whistling in his ear?
    He has fled to his blue ice-palace far
        On top of the world near the cold North Star.

Who has come to take his place?
    Sweet Spring is here with her smiling face,
    The warm West Wind blowing in her hair,
    Bluebirds and robins around her there.
    In her flowing gown of palest green
        She calls all the flowers to meet their Queen.

Who is the Queen so fair and bright,
Wearing a mantle of shining light,
Who follows the footsteps of smiling Spring
And sheds her warm light over everything?
    Roses and lilies will bloom for her
        For she is the bright Queen of Summer.

Who chases the Queen of Summer away?
    The fiery Dragon of Fall, they say.
    He burns all the leaves to red, orange, and brown,
    And with flaming breath he blows them down,
    Leaving the trees all cold and bare
    Till the snow of winter fills the air.

God's Gifts

Wherever human beings are,
'Neath Southern Cross or Northern Star,
On mountain top or sandy plain,
God's gifts to men are all the same.

Firm earth beneath their feet he gives,
In heavenly air man breathes and lives,
Fire warms him when the wild wind blows,
And for his thirst cool water flows.

Now stone and plant and beast and man
Have lived on earth since earth began,
And of all these 'tis man who gives
His thanks to God for all that lives.

Poem for C.K.

Every day I wake up and look out at the world,
For my windows are open and far do I see
The green earth, the blue sky, and the warm golden sun
Shining down on the mountains, the meadows and me.

Then I see all the colors of rainbows and flowers:
Violet, blue, green, and yellow and orange and red;
Birds with feathers so bright flying over the trees,
And below beasts that creep with a soft-footed tread.

When I open my windows to look at the world,
Other windows are there in the houses around,
And in them looking out other children I see,
And they call me to play with them down on the ground.

Poem for J.B.

The sweetest little flowers grow
In a secret place I know.
Fairies come there every morning
With their wands the flowers adorning,
Bringing sunshine to each flower,
Every day and every hour.

To each sunflower bowing down
The fairies give a golden crown.
Then every daisy near and far
Shines like a lovely morning star.
And when the fairies touch a rose,
A warm, red heart their wands disclose.

From my pretty, secret garden
Flowers I bring to all dear children:
That each one may have a part
From the garden of my heart.

Poem for R.D.

High mountains guard the valleys deep
Where tender flowers are growing,
And rocky cliffs so strong and steep
The gentle blossoms safely keep
When cold north winds are blowing.

Then let me be so firm and strong,
Just like the mountains high above,
That I'll keep watch the whole day long
And not let anything that's wrong
Hurt any of the friends I love.

Building Houses

This is the tepee the Indians built:
    This is the way they chop down the trees
    To get the poles for their tepees.
    This is the way, with arrow and bow,
    They hunt on the prairie for buffalo.
    This is the way they scrape off the hair
    To make the buffalo skins quite bare,
    Then sew them together, without any holes,
    To cover the frames of their tepee poles.

This is the house the Indians built
With adobe bricks and mortared with silt:
    This is the way they dig the trench
    To get the clay for wall and bench.
    This is the way they mix the clay:
    Earth and water and wisps of hay.
    This is the way they shape the bricks,
    Cutting the clay with flints and sticks.
    Row on row, in the blazing sun,
    They bake the bricks, but their work isn't done.
    When the bricks are hard, they build a wall
    And mortar each crack so it will not fall.
    Watery clay is their only plaster.
    Lift a brick, lay a brick, faster and faster,
    'Til all four walls, with window and door,
    Stand firm and strong 'round a plastered floor.
    Logs, as beams, on the walls are laid,

    And of slender poles the rafters are made.
    Then over it all more adobe is spread,
    'Til at last they have a roof overhead.

This is the house the Africans built:
    This is the way, in the jungle thick,
    They cut and hew both leaf and stick.
    This is the way they dig the holes
    In which to plant the upright poles.
    This is the way, with sticks and leaves,
    They weave the walls and tie the eaves.
    In and out the sticks they twine
    And tie them together with jungle vine.
    Then they cover the roof with leaves so wide
    That from it the raindrops will easily slide.

This is the tent the Nomads built:
    This is the way they shear the hair
    From all their goats with greatest care.
    This is the way they twist the threads
    With which to weave their tents and beds.
    This is the way, with warp and woof,
    They weave the blankets for floor and roof.
    This is the way they sew them together
    For shade and shelter in hottest weather.

This is the igloo the Eskimos built:
    This is the way they cut the snow
    In blocks so even, row on row.
    This is the way they build a wall
    Around in a circle so that it won't fall.
    Block after block of snow they heft,
    Upward and inward from right to left,
    Until the wall closes to make a round dome
    And the Eskimos find that they have a warm home
    Then they cut a hole through the wall of snow
    And make a door through which they can go.

The Number Four

As we are in the Fourth Grade, we like the number 4.
We find it all around us when we go out the door.

In 4 directions, we go forth:
East, West, South and North.

And 4 seasons bring to mind
The 4 kingdoms which we find
Of rocks, plants, animals and mankind.

They, in turn, exist and grow
Within 4 elements, as we know:
The solid earth, the spreading air
That bears the water and feeds the fire.

Back in our schoolroom now, we link
More 4s together to help us think.
By 4 processes in arithmetic, we
Count, weigh, measure, and that right quickly:
Subtraction, addition,
Multiplication, division.

And when we want to write a letter,
4 kinds of sentences make it better:
The question asks,
Statements reply,
Commands set tasks
Which exclamations defy!

But none of them would be well understood
If 4 punctuation marks weren't so helpful and good:
The question mark just has the task
Of ending all that questions ask.
There is the period who loves to rest;
All sentences stop at his request.
Then there's the comma, so nimble and busy;
Without him the sentences might make you dizzy.
Whatever the excitement rare,
The exclamation point is there.

Now, if you can enlarge on our story of 4,
We'll be glad to add a few verses more.

Four Kinds of Sentences

Imperative
Listen to the night wind blow.
See the swirling flakes of snow.
Close the window. Shut the door.
Keep out the wild wind's angry roar.
Light the fire. Let it blaze.
Warm the house with its hot rays.

Exclamatory
How wonderful the morning is!
Oh, what a sparkling day!
Sky's blue around the golden sun!
The wind has blown away!

Declarative
The golden sun shines on the snow.
The trees blue shadows make.
The colors of God's own rainbow
Twinkle in each snowflake.

Interrogative
Where do snowflakes come from?
Why are they so white?
Who gives them each a separate form?
How far has been their flight?
And what creates the rainbow
In each white star of snow?

The Four Elements

From snowy peak of mountain,
To green and level land,
The earth is shaped and hollowed
As by a mighty hand.

The silent peaks are lifted,
The valleys carved between,
The boundless plain is leveled
As by a hand unseen.

The hand of the Creator,
With flowing fire of will,
Reaching out to all things,
Raises up the hill.

The hand of the Creator,
In smoothing fall of rain,
Shapes the sloping valley,
Levels out the plain.

The love of the Creator,
Filling all the air,
Enfolding all creation,
Hovers everywhere.

The Earthworms

What do earthworms do by day?
Through sand and soil they eat their way.
What do earthworms do at night?
They search for food by the moon's pale light.

What do earthworms like to eat?
Decaying plants to them taste sweet,
And minerals that they have found
Five or six feet underground.

How do earthworms help us live?
New life to soil their castings give
That crops may flourish
Mankind to nourish.

Horses in the Rain

The rain flies down across the land
From Heaven's darkening height,
Bringing an early night,
While in the field the horses stand.

They are feeding in the pasture there,
Their big heads toward the ground,
Their legs like quiet roots earth-bound,
And on them falls the rainy air.

These are they who in the day
Do work and pull and go,
Always to and fro,
Wherever man doth say.

With hard foot and eager ear,
They follow man's commands
And feel his guiding hands,
Obeying every word they hear.

Now, in the rain and the night,
They stand and graze,
Far from man's ways,
Untouched and out of sight.

Mouse in the House

What are you looking for, little gray mouse,
As you hurry and scurry around the dark house?
Kind friend, I am hungry. Have you seen any cake,
In a crack or a corner, for me to take?

The Animals in Me

An eagle sees things from great height;
A lion's heart is strong;
An antelope is fleet in flight;
Wisdom, courage, and good will
In me belong.

The Lion's Pride

There was a pride of lions who
Were never captured for a zoo.

No one had to bring them meat!
They caught it running on swift feet.

With bared fangs and outstretched claws,
They sprang and pranced and closed their jaws.

Giraffe or zebra was no more
Once it heard a lion roar!

The lion is the King of Beasts.
No one dares disturb his feasts.

We say cattle graze in "herds."
We speak of "flocks" of sheep or birds,

A "pack" of jackals, "swarms" of bees.
One lion's worth the lot of these.

His dignity cannot be denied.
That's why his group is called a "pride."

The Wheat and the Bread

"Give us this day our daily bread,"
Is the prayer which to our Lord is said.
And we can see in the grain of wheat
The beginning of the bread we eat.
A figure 8 at one end of the grain,
Warmed by sun, softened by rain,
Grows up toward the sun and down through the ground
Like a musical scale that gives no sound.
Warmed by the sun and washed by the rain,
Green wheat turns into golden grain.
The grain is cut and winnowed and ground
As the millstones turn around and around
To make the flour which is sifted fine,
To be mixed with water and sugar and brine
And milk, and the yeast that makes the bread rise,
So that, in the oven, we find a surprise:
The crusty loaves, all golden brown,
Which feed all the people in every town.

Verses for Children

The sun's warmth brings beauty to the earth,
So my heart's feeling can find beauty everywhere.
The sun's light finds the hidden seed,
So the light of my thinking can find the hidden truth.
The sun's power awakens all that sleeps,
So my will awakens me to deeds.

        ಃ   ಃ   ಃ

Noble and lofty is the Oak,
The king of trees.
Around its powerful roots
The tiny moss is also great and good,
Gathering the moisture which the Oak's root needs.
Whether large or small,
All beings who are true to their own nature
Can be great and good.

        ಃ   ಃ   ಃ

Invisibly within the seed
The plant is waiting for its days of growth.
Root, stern, and leaf, the flower and fruit
Will sprout and bloom and ripen
As the sun and rain call them forth.
So, life will call from me
What now invisibly is waiting.

        ಃ   ಃ   ಃ

Springing up, winging upward, nesting high
Away from earth, the birds are creatures of the sky.
My home is on the ground where I stand
And walk with firmly stepping feet.

        ಃ   ಃ   ಃ

Only from what is true
Can I draw the strength
To stand in life bravely,
To go through life untroubled.
I must always know the truth.

The Prince Who Could Not Read

Once upon a time, there was a little Prince. When he was old enough, his father, the King, said to him, "Tomorrow you start going to school where you will learn not only how to read and write and count, but also those things that will help you to be a good king when I am gone."

The Prince had no brothers or sisters to play with, and when he arrived at school the next morning and saw all the other boys and girls, only one thought filled his mind. Now he would have someone to play with. Every morning thereafter, he set out for school full of joy at the thought of seeing the other children. His father, the King, was pleased to see how happy his son was.

Little did the King imagine the truth as to what his son was learning in school. He was a busy king, so concerned for the welfare of his subjects that he had little time to worry about his son. Thus it was that, year after year for three whole years, the Prince went happily to school before the King took time to see how well his son was able to read.

After supper one evening, the King wrote out a little verse on a scrap of paper:

> Work while you work
> And play while you play;
> That is the way to be
> Happy and gay.

Then he asked his son to read the verse. The Prince looked at the writing and was perfectly silent. "Well," said the King, "what is the first word?"

"Krow–" mumbled the Prince.

"You are reading it backward," said the King. He had to help his son read the word from left to right. "W-o-r-k spells work," said the King.

It took a long time to help the Prince find out what the next two words were, but at last he could repeat, "Work while you—"

"Now," said the King, "what is the fourth word?"

"Krow," answered the Prince.

The King didn't even try to help the Prince read the rest of the verse. Instead, the next day, he went to the schoolroom and hid himself behind a screen where he could see and hear everything that went on in his son's class without being seen himself. What he did see made him feel most anxious: While the teacher was teaching, the Prince was making faces at the other children, trying to get them to laugh at him. And when the teacher gave them some writing to do, the Prince, instead of writing, was playing with his pencils and trying to build a house with them. And when the rest of the class was reading, the Prince kept getting up from his desk and running to look out the window whenever a bird flew by. No wonder he wasn't learning his lessons!

Sad at heart, the King stepped from behind the screen, took the Prince by the hand, and led him away from the school. When they reached the royal palace, the King spoke thus to his son: "Anyone who has to be king someday and to rule over other people must first learn to rule over himself. You have been in school for three years, but you have not learned to pay attention to instruction, to work instead of play, and to keep your mind on one thing at a time. So I must send you out into the world to learn these lessons. When you have learned them, you may come home again but not before! I would rather have no son than to have one who cannot rule himself."

Whereupon the King gave the Prince a loaf of bread and a jug of water and sent him out into the world.

Alone and without friends or money, the Prince traveled on foot for many days until his loaf of bread was eaten. When he came to a village, he found a baker's shop. He went in and asked for a loaf of bread.

"Well now," said the baker, "you look like a fine, strong lad! If you will stay here and work for me, you may have all the bread you can eat."

Being very hungry, the Prince agreed to work for the baker, who gave him some bread and milk and then asked him to help put the new bread in the oven. The dough was all mixed and shaped into loaves, and they put the loaves on big trays and then lifted the trays into the oven. Whereupon the baker told the Prince to watch the baking while he went home to supper. He told the Prince to take the bread out of the oven when it was as brown as a walnut shell, and no browner.

Alone in the baker's shop, the Prince looked around and saw all the baker's shovels standing against the oven walls and a supply of firewood heaped in the corner of the shop. *Well,* thought the Prince, *these will be good to play with!*

So he set to work to build a house with them, stacking them up on each other to make four walls, a door, a window and a roof. All this took quite a long while, and as the Prince laid the last shovel on the roof, he smelled smoke and saw it pouring out between the cracks of the oven door.

Just then the baker came back. He saw the Prince. He saw the play house made of shovels and firewood. Yet more clearly he saw the smoke curling out through the cracks of the oven door, and with a shout, he dashed to the oven and threw open the door. "You've let the bread burn!" he roared.

The Prince had forgotten all about the bread while he was playing, but now he remembered. Looking into the oven, he saw that every loaf was burnt as black as a cinder.

"A whole day's work gone up in smoke!" wept the baker. "Now I'll have to work all night. And all this because of your child's play! Get out. Be on your way. I've had enough of you." Then he pushed the Prince out of the shop and locked the door behind him.

All night long, under the stars and moon, the young Prince traveled, not knowing where he was going. By morning he had reached another town and was very hungry for some breakfast. He knocked at the door of a house, and when it was opened, he saw that it was a shoemaker's shop. He asked the shoemaker for some breakfast.

"Well now," said the shoemaker, "you look like a fine, strong lad. If you'll stay here and work for me, I'll give you breakfast, dinner, tea and supper every day."

The Prince agreed to stay, and the shoemaker gave him some breakfast and then the job of waxing the thread with which he sewed the shoes. It wasn't a hard job, and the Prince worked at it quite steadily until the shoemaker happened to leave the room. Then the Prince stopped working and looked around.

The shop was full of so many interesting things: all sorts of tools, nails, pieces of leather, and different kinds of shoes in all shapes and colors—dancing shoes, walking shoes, work shoes, and slippers—and in a minute the Prince was up and away from his workbench, running from one corner of the room to another, looking at everything on shelf and table and even in cupboard and drawer!

When the shoemaker came back and found the Prince playing with a box of nails, he said, "Come now, get busy with that thread. I can't sew up my shoes without it."

Yet, the next time the shoemaker left the room, the Prince was up and around looking again at everything he hadn't noticed before.

To make a long story short, the day was not over before the shoemaker was out of thread and couldn't finish his day's work because the Prince had spent more time looking around than waxing the thread. The shoemaker saw that the Prince was no worker. "I can only feed someone who will work and help me finish my shoes on time," said the shoemaker, and once again the Prince was turned out of the house.

He traveled all night, under the stars and moon, not knowing where he was going. In the morning, when he was again hungry for some breakfast, he found himself near a big farm. He went up to the farmer's house and asked for some food.

"Well now," said the farmer, "you look like a good, strong lad. If you will stay here and help us cut the hay, I'll be glad to give you your meals and a bed to sleep in." So, the Prince agreed to help the farmer cut the hay.

Now there were some other boys the Prince's age, who were there to help the farmer cut his hay. After breakfast, he gave them each a sickle and drove them out to the field to work. He showed them how much hay they were to cut and load onto the wagon before noon, then left them to get on with it while he went to another field to harvest the wheat.

All did not go well! In fact, it was the Prince's fault, for he had not yet learned his lesson. As soon as he was left alone with the other boys, he wanted to play instead of work. First he made faces at them, and funny noises, to make them laugh at him. Then when they had cut a little hay and tossed it up on the hay wagon, the Prince climbed up on the wagon and threw the hay down on the boys. This started a hay fight, and it was lots of fun, more fun than the Prince had had since he'd left school. The hay flew fast. The boys on one side of the wagon threw the hay back at those on the other side. Just as the hay was flying fastest up over the wagon and back, the farmer appeared.

Of course, when he saw what was going on, he didn't waste any time. He chased those boys away with his pitchfork, shouting, "Get out of there, you good-for-nothing rapscallions, or I'll skin you alive."

Now the boys weren't as gay and friendly as they had been, and all of them chased after the Prince, throwing sticks and stones and yelling that it was his fault they'd gotten into trouble. The Prince ran as fast as he could and finally left them behind. Now he was alone once more, without food or shelter.

Night came, and just as the stars and moon appeared, he saw a little hut nearby. The door was open. When no one answered his knock, he went in and the door slammed shut behind him. The hut was bare. There were no chairs, no table, no bed—nothing but four walls and a dirt floor. It was cold, he was hungry, the night was dark, and not a sound could be heard. The Prince was very much alone.

He sat on the ground and began to think. He thought about the farmer. He thought about the shoemaker. He thought about the baker. He thought of his school. He thought of his father and remembered what his father had said: "I would rather have no son than one who cannot rule himself."

Then the poor Prince sighed and cried, "If only I had cut the hay or waxed the thread or watched the bread, I could have some supper.

Then he sighed again and cried, "If only I had learned to read, I could have stayed in my father's palace."

He sobbed and moaned aloud and did not hear the sound of little feet tramping toward the door. The door opened. In came a tiny man carrying a lantern. He held the light up to the Prince's face. "What's the matter with you?" he asked. The Prince said he was hungry and wanted to go home.

"Tell me, where is your home?" asked the little man. He had a long white beard and sparkling eyes, and he looked so interested that the Prince could not keep from telling him about all that had happened, and then he burst into tears again, crying "I want to go home!"

"From what you tell me," said the dwarf wisely, "I can see that the only way you can do that is to go the same way that you came here, and this time if you cut the hay and wax the thread and watch the bread, you'll find yourself at home before you know it."

So the young Prince took the little man's advice and went back to the farmer and the shoemaker and the baker, and at each place, he humbled himself and begged for forgiveness, saying "Let me work for you for a year and a day, and you'll never be sorry."

In each place, he stayed a year and a day. Never before had the farmer, the shoemaker, and the baker had such a good helper. Not one of them wanted to let him leave, but when he said, "I must go home to my father, the King," they were filled with wonder and let him go.

After the three years and three days were over, the Prince came home. His father, the King, was overjoyed to see him, for he knew that the Prince wouldn't have come back unless he had learned to rule himself.

And sure enough, the Prince went back to school and paid attention to his teachers and soon learned to read and write and even count. But more than that, he proved to his father that he was worthy to be a king when his time came.

And when the old King died, he was happy that he could leave his kingdom to such a worthy son.

As soon as the Prince was crowned King, he sent for the baker, the shoemaker, and the farmer and made them his closest counselors. They all lived to a good, old age and ruled the kingdom wisely and well.

The Secret and Magic Name of the King

In a far country, there ruled a good king. He was wise and kind, and all of his people loved him. One day, he called his son to him and said, "Someday you will be king in my place. Then you will have to be as wise as I am. You will have to know the secret and magic name of the king."

Then the Prince said, "Who will teach me that, Father?"

And his father answered, "There is only one person who is allowed to tell you that, and that person is myself, for I myself am King. But if I should die before I tell you the secret and magic name, then you would have to find it out for yourself."

The Prince said, "Tell me now, Father."

The King replied, "This is not the time, for I am still young and will be king for many years to come. When I am old and near to death, then I will tell you."

Not long after this, the King went riding on his horse through the hills and forests of his kingdom to visit his people and see whether they were all happy and well-fed. On his way home toward evening, he rode through a dark wood. Some hunters did not see the King riding on his horse, but they heard the sound of his horse's hooves trampling the ground over leaves and twigs. Thinking it was a bear, they shot their arrows toward the sound. One arrow struck the King, piercing his heart, so that he fell from his horse and died before the frightened hunters could help him. Great was their grief as they carried him tenderly to his palace. They asked the wise men of the kingdom to punish them, to take their lives if necessary. Knowing it was an accident, the wise men only pitied the hunters and told them that their sorrow was their punishment.

So it was that the good King died before he had a chance to tell his son the secret and magic name of the king. The wise men summoned the Prince and asked, "Do you know the secret and magic name of the king?"

"No," said the Prince. "My father died before he could tell me."

"Then," said the wise men, "you will have to find it out for yourself before you can wear the king's crown and sit on the royal throne."

The next morning, before the sun was up, the young Prince set forth to journey in search of the secret and magic name of the king, never to return home until he had found it. After walking many miles, he came to a wide river, over which there was no bridge. A boat stood near the shore, so he went over to it, and there in the boat sat an old, old man with a long white beard. "Can you take me across the river?" asked the Prince.

The old man said not a word but motioned to the Prince to get into the boat. As soon as the Prince stepped in, the old man took up his oars and with great strong arms rowed swiftly across the river. He looked so wise that the Prince thought he must know the secret and magic name of the king. When they reached the other shore, the Prince paid the ferryman and then said, "I am traveling in search of the secret and magic name of the king. Do you know where I can learn of it?"

The old man looked sharply at the Prince, then pointed to a distant mountain and answered:

> The King of the Rocks in the mountain sleeps,
> While the Tree King dreams in the dark woods deep,
> And the King of Beasts through the forests creeps.

More than this he would not say. And so, the Prince thanked him and journeyed to the mountain.

The mountain was rocky and its sides were steep, so steep that a human being could not climb them without falling down. Great pillars of rock stood straight up like the columns of a great palace, and sure enough, between the great columns he saw a dark and narrow opening. Bravely he went in and found that he could walk on. It was so dark that he had to put his hands out before him and feel his way. All the sounds of the world—the singing of birds, the buzzing of insects, the wind blowing through leaves—all these sounds were gone, and in the pitch-dark passageway, the Prince went deeper and deeper, into the very middle of the mountain.

Suddenly, he saw a glimmering light, and as he hurried toward it, the passageway grew broader and then widened out into a great cavern, which was the throne room of the King of the Rocks, and there he sat on a great rock throne. He was as big as a giant, so big that the Prince could hardly see his head and face. At his feet lay piles and piles of precious stones all shining with a flickering light, and in and out among the heaps of precious stones, little gnomes were hurrying, bringing in more jewels from various other passageways to pile them up at the feet of the King of the Rocks. In their caps, the gnomes each wore a little light, and over their shoulders, they each carried a tiny pick-axe, for they were miners who dug the most precious of stones out of the earth for the King.

Looking up at the King, the Prince could just barely see that his eyes were shut as if he were asleep. In fact, the King never moved. He was made of stone. Only the busy gnomes were awake. As soon as they noticed the Prince, they crowded around him in a very friendly way. Some offered him jewels; others danced for him; others did cartwheels and somersaults to show off. One gave him his pick-axe, another his cap with the little light burning in it. Then they all tried to pull him with them—off to dig in the mountain.

The Prince cried out, "I have come to see the King!" Then he bowed low before the King and said, "Your Majesty, can you tell me the secret and magic name of the king?"

The great King of the Rocks made no answer. His eyes were still shut. The little gnomes danced and rolled over each other, laughing and whispering among themselves. They sounded like whispering waters. They sounded as if they were saying, "He sleeps, he sleeps, he sleeps."

"Will he never wake up?" cried the Prince.

And the little gnomes jumped and rolled and laughed and whispered, "He sleeps, he sleeps, he sleeps."

Then the Prince remembered what the ferryman had said: "The King of the Rocks in the mountain sleeps." A sleeping king could never tell him the secret and magic name. Waving goodbye to the friendly gnomes who were already busy at their work again, the Prince went back the way he had come, until once more he stood out in the light of day.

He decided to look for the next king, the Tree King. Surely this king would not be a sleeper. He traveled for many a day until he came to a great forest. There, among the trees of the forest, he wandered, wondering how to find the King of the Trees. While he was thus wandering and wondering, he came upon a beautiful forest glade where the thick woods opened out and all the trees stood in a large circle around a great oak tree. Around its roots, the grass was soft, and green. Many beautiful wildflowers blossomed in rainbow colors all through the grass and crowded around Oak Tree's roots—or were they feet? Yes, they looked like great feet standing among the flowers! There, too, among the flowers and grass blades, swarms of Sun Fairies circle, weaving a mantle of sunshine to help the plants grow.

The Prince looked up at the great Oak Tree. This was the King of Trees, his feet rooted in the earth, his branching arms stretching upward, his great leafy head reaching far and high into the blue sky. And up there in the air a band of angels circled in a slow and graceful dance, building the King's crown out of rays of golden sunlight. It all seemed like a beautiful dream. Kneeling respectfully before the Tree King, the Prince asked, "Your Majesty, can you tell me the secret and magic name of the king?"

He heard the oak leaves whispering in the wind, but no other sound. The great King of the Trees gave no answer as the angels moved slowly above his head to make his shining crown. Once again, the Prince remembered what the old ferryman had said: "The Tree King dreams in the dark woods deep." So this king, too, could give no answer, for he lived in a dream and could not hear the Prince's question.

The Prince did not have to go far to find the King of the Beasts, for he ruled his kingdom in this very forest, and even stalked through the kingdom of the Tree King without waking him from his dream. As the Prince stood there in the forest glade, the King of Beasts marched by. Such a mighty beast was he, a glorious golden beast with a flaming mane of yellow hair for his crown. From before him fled many an animal of the forest, running as fast as it could, for fear of being caught and eaten. But the lion had already had his dinner and wasn't hungry. So he lay down under the Tree King among the flowers and the Sun Fairies and looked at the Prince as he licked his paws and cleaned his whiskers.

"This king neither sleeps nor dreams," thought the Prince, "so perhaps he can hear and speak." Whereupon he walked over and bowed before the King of Beasts and said, "Your Majesty, can you tell me the secret and magic name of the king?"

And the King of the Beasts said, "Gr-r-r-r-r-r," and he said, "Br-r-r-r-r-r," and he said, "Mr-r-r-r-r-r," but not a word could he speak.

So the Prince turned away from him and left the forest, sad at heart, for he had not learned the secret and could not return to his own kingdom without it. He wept tears of grief as he thought of his father, and he felt that no one could be as lonely as he was.

He stood before the river once more, the wide river with no bridge across it. The ferry boat was waiting near the shore. The old, old man was standing in it, and he beckoned to the Prince with his hand. As soon as the Prince stepped into the boat, the old man began to row with his strong arms, and the boat moved swiftly across the river.

"Where are you taking me?" asked the Prince. On the other side of the river he saw his father's palace shining in the sunlight. The ferryman said not a word.

"I can't go home yet," cried the Prince. "The King of the Rocks sleeps, the Tree King dreams, and the King of Beasts can only growl. But I am neither rock, nor tree, nor beast. I am—"

"That's it!" shouted the old man rowing harder than ever, and the boat jumped ahead.

"I!" called the Prince. "I am—king!"

"Yes, yes," cried the old man. "You have found your name, the secret and magic name of the king!"

"I?" asked the Prince.

"Yes," said the wise, old man as his boat touched the shore. "Only you can call yourself by that name. It is the name you can give to no one else but yourself."

The Prince hurried home and presented himself to the wise men who had been ruling his kingdom for him. To them he said, "Bring me the crown of the King and seat me on the King's throne, for I am the King!"

The Princess of the Golden Stairs

Once upon a time, a King had three sons. The oldest one, who would by rights become king someday in his father's place, was big and strong and always took for himself the best of everything: the best horse, the softest bed, and the biggest plate of food. He had no use for his younger brothers. Whenever they went anywhere together, he always pushed them out of the way so that he could be first.

The second son was quite small and thin, but he was clever and quick. He knew how to count up to a thousand, how to read big, thick books, and he thought that he would make a much better king than his older brother, if only something would happen to make that possible. So he spent a great deal of time plotting as to how he could win the King's crown for himself.

The youngest son was not big and strong, nor was he clever, but he had a good heart and always thought of others before he thought of himself. He did not imagine that he would ever be as important as the oldest brother or as clever as the second brother. He was fond of the poorest horse in the King's stable. He slept on the hardest bed quite comfortably, and he ate what was left after his brothers had taken what they wanted.

One day the three brothers went hunting. They set out early in the morning just as the sun was rising. The oldest brother was riding the finest of the King's horses, the second brother rode the next best horse, while the third brother followed behind on a poor beast who was too old to run fast, but who, nevertheless, was very gentle and steady.

As they thus approached a great forest, a beautiful white deer sprang up from the bushes and ran off into the forest. The two older brothers spurred their swift horses after it and soon disappeared among the trees, leaving the youngest brother to follow as best he could on his poor, old horse.

For many hours he followed their trail, looking for the marks of their horses' hooves on the forest paths. The day passed in this way until, as the sun was setting, the youngest brother heard voices in the woods. Riding toward the voices, at last he came upon the other two sitting by a fire they had made to keep themselves warm. There they had prepared to spend the night, for they were quite lost in the dismal forest. Nor had they caught up with the white deer that had led them into the wild woods.

The oldest brother made the other two give him their coats to keep him warm. Rolling up in them, he was soon comfortably asleep. The second brother then took the best place by the fire, where the smoke from the fire would not blow in his face, and he told the youngest brother that he was to keep the fire going all night. Thus, the second brother went to sleep on a comfortable bed of pine boughs while the youngest brother spent the whole night gathering wood for the fire.

As soon as the sun came up the next morning, the two older brothers woke up. They said not a word to the youngest to thank him for keeping the fire going all night long. In fact, they mounted their horses and set out to find their way home, leaving the youngest to put out the fire and follow as best he could on his poor, old horse.

As they were all three riding along not knowing where their path led, they came upon a small hut. The oldest brother pushed ahead and banged on the door. It was quickly opened by a little old man with a long, white beard that reached to his knees. Without waiting to be invited, the oldest brother pushed his way into the hut. Then while the little old man's back was turned, the second brother sneaked in. The youngest, meanwhile, waited outside until he should be invited in. He waited quite a while.

Now what was going on inside the hut? Once inside, the oldest brother saw a small table, and on the table a bowl of hot porridge, the old man's meal. Immediately, he ate it all up. The second brother, looking in all the corners of the hut, found a sack of applies. He helped himself to these. The little old man said not a word but stood watching them with his bright, blue eyes.

After the two had eaten everything up, the oldest said in a loud voice, "I am the eldest son of the King. Someday I will be the King. My foolish brothers are with me, lost in the forest, old man, and perhaps you can show us the way we must go to return to our palace." Whereupon, the little man answered:

> The way to go
> You soon will know
> When, in this hidden place,
> You see your hidden face."

"What riddle is this?" shouted the oldest prince. "Explain it to me or I'll tear you limb from limb."

Then said the old man, "To find your way out of this magic wood will be possible only if you have the courage to see yourself as you really are."

"Ho, ho!" shouted the prince. "Courage? I have more than enough of that."

"Where may we have this pleasure?" asked the second brother.

The old man led them out behind the hut to a covered well. Slowly he lifted off the cover and told the princes to look in.

The oldest brother was pleased at the thought of seeing himself as he really was. Surely he would see himself wearing a king's robe and a golden crown. But when he looked into the well, he turned pale. Looking up at him through the clear water was a savage wolf, with open jaws and sharp teeth, ready to leap at him and devour him. He jumped back quickly, but then pretended that nothing had happened. "I can see that my hair needs combing," he said. "That is the only thing that is wrong."

The second brother took his turn, thinking what a pleasure it would be to see himself wearing a king's robe and a golden crown. But when he looked into the well, he turned green. Looking up at him through the clear water was a sly fox, crouching as if ready to pounce on him. He too stepped back quickly and pretended that nothing unusual had happened. "All that I can see is that my cloak is wrinkled," said he.

Meanwhile the youngest brother had followed them, and the little old man beckoned to him to look into the well. This he did, and there, in the water, he saw a gentle, little white lamb who gazed up at him with loving eyes as if pleading with him to take it with him. He reached for it, but before he could catch hold of it, the little man put the cover over the well. No sooner had this happened than the whole magic wood vanished into thin air, and with it the little old man, the hut, the well, and all! And the princes found themselves at the gate of their father's palace.

The two older brothers kept what they had seen a dark secret, even from each other. But they could not forget. The oldest kept thinking of the savage wolf. Every day he looked in the mirror and should have been comforted to see his own face looking back at him, for it did. Yet he was not comforted. What if, suddenly, he would turn into a wolf in front of other people? He began to wear long, velvet robes that hid his arms and legs and large, drooping hats with big plumes that fell over his shoulders and hid his face. The second brother, likewise, kept looking at himself in mirrors. He seldom left his own room for fear he would change into a fox while walking about, and thus be shot by the King's guards.

As for the third brother, he remembered the little lamb and wished he could have brought it home with him, but he never told anyone about it because he didn't imagine that anyone would be interested.

Now at this time there lived, in a neighboring kingdom, a most beautiful princess whose fame had spread far and wide. Not only was she more beautiful than any other princess, but she could paint beautiful pictures and sing sweet songs, and she was full of knowledge and wisdom. She lived in a golden palace at the top of a steep, rocky mountain. Leading up to this palace—the only way of reaching it at all—was a golden stairway that shone like the sun.

Now the word was sent out that the Princess would marry the prince who could climb up the golden stairs without leaving a single mark or scratch upon them, so that they would shine as brightly as ever after he had passed.

Hearing of this, the King called his three sons to him and said, "Whichever one of you can win this wonderful princess for your wife shall be the king when I am dead, for she is so great that any man who had her as his wife would certainly be the best king."

The King's oldest son immediately threw off his long robe and plumed hat and rushed to the stable where he saddled the best horse and set off to find and win the Princess of the Golden Stairs.

On the way, he saw a little white lamb that was trying to swim across a deep river. The lamb cried out for help because the current was too strong. The Prince laughed at it and shouted, "I have better things to do." And he galloped away. Then he met a fox that had been wounded by a hunter. Limping painfully along, it begged for help and water. The Prince laughed at it and shouted, "I have better things to do." And he galloped away. Farther on, he saw a wolf caught in a trap. The wolf begged to be freed and promised that he would help the Prince in return. At the sight of the wolf, the Prince was enraged, set an arrow in his bow, and shot at the wolf. Then he galloped away shouting, "I have better things to do."

At last he saw the golden stairs leading to the golden palace high at the top of the steep, rocky mountain. He got off his horse and put soft, thick stockings over his shoes so that as he climbed the stairs, he would leave no mark upon them. Then up he went, step after step without looking back, until he stood before the golden gates of the palace. They were closed.

He pulled a golden cord, and far inside he heard the chime of a bell. Then all was silent. He pulled the cord again, and again, the bell chimed, and again there was silence. Then he pounded on the gate with his fists, and while he was yet pounding he heard a voice call out, "Look behind you and see where you have stepped."

Looking back, the Prince saw that in spite of his soft, thick stockings, every one of his footprints showed on the golden stairs as dark and red as blood. Alas! Knowing that he could not win the Princess, he went away and was never heard of again.

Meanwhile, the King's second son had set out, almost on the heels of his older brother and traveled almost as fast. He too saw the little white lamb struggling and crying out for help in the swift river current, but he left it to drown saying, "There are too many lambs in the world anyway." He met the wounded fox that was begging for help and water, but he shot at it and galloped away saying, "You'll never bother me again." And when he passed the wolf caught in a trap and begging for its freedom, the Prince thought only of his older brother and spurred his horse on to try to get ahead of him.

When at last he too reached the golden stairs leading to the golden palace at the top of the steep, rocky mountain, they were shining as brightly as the sun. He got off his horse and laid a soft piece of carpet on the first step. Standing on this, he placed a second carpet on the second step. And so he climbed the golden stairs, picking up the carpet behind him and setting it ahead of him, until he reached the golden gates of the palace.

As they were closed, he pulled the golden cord and heard the chime of the bell. Then all was silent. For a second time, he pulled the cord, again the bell chimed, and again there was silence. He began to jerk the bell cord, over and over again, and while the bell was yet chiming, a voice called out, "Look behind you and see where you have stepped."

Looking back, the second brother saw that the golden steps were marked with dirt and dust. Alas! He knew the golden gates would not open for him, and he too went away and was never heard from again.

Meanwhile, the youngest brother had not planned to seek the hand of the Princess of the Golden Stairs. But his father told him that he must so that he would have a fair chance to be king. So he made preparations and set forth on his gentle, old horse to follow the path taken by his older brothers through the fields and forests.

As he approached a deep river, he saw a little white lamb trying to swim across the swift current and crying out for help. The Prince dismounted and swam out to the drowning creature and brought it safely to shore. Then he placed it in front of him on his horse and took it along as a gift for the Princess.

When he saw the wounded fox limping along and begging for help and water, he again dismounted, bound up its wound, and gave it water. And when he came upon the suffering wolf, he set it free from the trap.

When at length, he reached the golden stairway leading up to the golden palace at the top of the steep, rocky mountain, he was filled with wonder at its beauty. Lifting the little lamb to his shoulder, he did not even think to take off his shoes, which were caked with river mud, before he climbed the stairs. When he reached the palace gates, he pulled the golden bell cord, and while the bell was yet chiming, the gates swung open and he went in.

Wonder of wonders, behind him each step of the golden stairway was shining like the sun!

So it was that the youngest son of the King won the hand of the beautiful Princess of the Golden Stairs and took her home as his bride. And when his father died, he became the King with the Princess as his Queen, and they ruled the kingdom wisely and well.

The Soldier, the Huntsman and the Servant

Once there was a young king who ruled over a great kingdom. As he had no queen, his counselors begged him to find a wife so that he might in time have a son to rule over the kingdom when he should die. But the young king refused. "For," he said, "women are silly, stubborn creatures who think only of themselves, and a wife would only bring me trouble."

Nevertheless the counselors continued to beseech him to marry, and they gave him no peace until be finally said, "Very well, I will marry any woman who, disguised as a man, can serve me for a year and a day without my discovering her." Immediately, the proclamation was sent out:

"Any maiden who, disguised as a man, can serve the King for a year and a day without being discovered, shall at the end of that time become Queen."

Now it happened that in this kingdom there was a poor widow who had three daughters. The oldest was proud and stubborn. She thought only of herself and would never do anything that she didn't want to do. Whenever she was asked to help her poor mother, she would stamp her feet, toss her head, curl her lip, and say, "Why should I? I don't want to!" or "No, I won't."

The second daughter spent most of her time changing her clothes and fixing her hair in front of a mirror. Her mother could get no help from her in the housework because this daughter would leave the bread to burn, the beds unmade, and the floors unswept while she posed and primped in front of the mirror.

So it was that the youngest daughter did more than her share of the housework, but she did it well and did whatever she was told without complaint. She cooked and cleaned, seeded the garden, and chopped firewood with an axe. She learned to do all the work that a man can do and grew to be strong of arm. Often the mother would say, "If it weren't for my youngest, I don't know how we would get along for she can do all the work that a man can do, and she is like a son to me."

Now when the two older daughters heard of the King's proclamation, each one immediately made up her mind that she would be queen. So the oldest one disguised herself as a soldier and went to seek service with the King. The second one dressed herself as a huntsman and likewise went to serve the King.

Their mother was only too glad to let them go, for it meant that there were two mouths less to feed, and they had never been any help or comfort to her. But when she saw her youngest daughter working day after day without thought for herself, the mother said, "Why shouldn't you be queen someday? You'd make a fine queen!"

At first the youngest daughter said, "No! I will stay with you and take care of you."

Then the mother said, "If you became queen, all of our troubles would end." Thus she persuaded her. The youngest daughter then dressed herself as a common serving-man and went to the King's court to become his servant.

In this way, all three sisters entered the King's service. The oldest, dressed as a soldier, carried a sword and shield and stood next to the King in public to protect him from his enemies. The second, dressed as a huntsman, carried a bow and arrows and followed the King when he went hunting. Dressed as a common servant, the youngest polished the King's armor, fed his horse, and cooked the King's food.

Nearly a year passed, and as yet the King had not discovered that the soldier, the huntsman, and the servant were in reality women. But near the end of the year, something happened. The King heard of a great treasure in a faraway, wild country—gold, silver and precious stones in huge amounts—which was stored in a mountain cave and guarded by a fierce dragon with nine heads. The King made up his mind that he would capture this treasure, and rather than take his whole army with him, he decided to take only a few picked men to help him conquer the dragon. So he chose one soldier, one huntsman, and one servant. Strange to say, these three were none other than the three sisters.

As they set out on their journey, the King rode forth first on a beautiful, snow-white horse. Then came the soldier, carrying sword and shield, and riding a coal-black horse. Next came the huntsman, dressed in green, carrying his bow and arrows, and riding a brown horse. Last of all came the servant riding on a mule and carrying an axe with which to cut firewood in the forest.

At the end of the first day, when they stopped to camp for the night, the King said to the soldier, "You are the one to fight the dragon." To the huntsman, he said, "You are the one to hunt in the forest for meat that we may eat tonight." To the servant, he said, "You are the one to make the fire and cook the meat."

At this, the huntsman acted very strangely. He giggled and jumped up and down in great excitement so that his bow slipped off his shoulder into some bushes. Then his cap fell off as he hunted madly for his bow, and he had to look for his cap. The arrows fell out of his quiver and were scattered over the ground. It took him quite some time to find and arrange everything again. But before he put on his cap, he took a comb and a mirror from his knapsack. Propping the mirror against the branch of a tree, he stood in front of it and combed his hair very nicely before putting on his cap.

The King, who was impatient for his dinner, flew into a rage and was just about to give the huntsman a blow with his fist when he paused. Taking a piece of paper from one of his saddle bags, he wrote something on it, then folded it and sealed it. Giving it to the huntsman he said, "I can see that you will be of no help as a huntsman. Take this message back to the counselors at my palace without fail, on pain of death."

So it was that the huntsman returned to the King's palace and delivered the paper to the King's counselors. When they opened it, they read:

> This huntsman so fine
> Will be no Queen of mine.
> She's just a silly girl,
> So put her to work as a palace maid
> And let her sweep the floors.

Thus the second daughter was discovered and had to spend the rest of her days sweeping the floors in the King's palace. In the meantime, the King, the soldier, and the servant traveled on, and it was the servant who now not only made the fire and cooked, but hunted for meat as well.

At last one day, they drew near to the dragon's mountain. They could hear the dragon roar, they could feel the earth shake under his mighty tread, and they could see clouds of smoke and flame rising in the air near the top of the mountain.

Now the King said to the soldier, "You are the one to fight the dragon, so sharpen your sword and mount your horse and advance against the dragon. We will follow to give you aid should you need it."

Then the soldier acted strangely. He stamped his feet on the ground, tossed his head, curled his lip, and said, "Why should I? I don't want to!"

Whereupon the King said, "I am the King! You are my soldier. You are bound to do as I say."

"Oh, no, I won't," answered the soldier.

This put the King in a great rage, and he was just about to give the soldier a blow with his fist when he paused, took a piece of paper from one of his saddle bags and wrote on it. Then he folded the paper, sealed it, and said to the soldier, "Since you are no help as a soldier, take this message back to my counselors without fail, on pain of death."

The soldier, more than happy not to have to fight the dragon, rode away. When he finally delivered the King's message to the King's counselors, they opened it and read:

> This soldier so fine
> Will be no Queen of mine.
> She's just a stubborn girl,
> So put her to work in the scullery
> And let her wash the dishes."

Thus the oldest daughter was discovered and had to spend the rest of her days washing dishes.

In the meantime, the King was left to face the dragon alone with his faithful servant who said, "Let me go first to strike at the dragon with my axe, and while the dragon struggles with me, you can creep up behind him and safely slay him."

The King agreed to this. While the servant swung his axe in front of the nine fire-breathing heads of the dragon, the King came upon him from behind and chopped off the heads one by one. So they won the treasure. As a reward, the King gave his servant a beautiful gold chain to wear around his neck.

Now it was just a year and a day since the youngest sister had dressed herself as a servant and entered the King's service, but she did not reveal herself, and after they returned to the palace, she disappeared.

The King, however, had learned to love his faithful servant. When he disappeared, the King was so sad that he dressed himself as a poor peasant and traveled from place to place in search of his beloved helper.

Thus he came to a poor widow's hut one evening and begged to be sheltered there for the night. The woman let him come in and told him to warm himself at the fire. Then she called out to someone in the kitchen, "Daughter, cook another potato, for we have a guest who will share our supper with us."

When it was time to eat, the King sat down at the table with the poor woman. From the kitchen came her daughter carrying a big bowl of baked potatoes and wearing around her neck a beautiful golden chain. As soon as the King saw the chain, he jumped to his feet and, in great excitement, looked at the girl. Then he saw that her hair and her eyes were of the same color as those of his lost servant. With great joy, he revealed that he was the King, and he begged her to become his Queen. "For," he said, "you are as strong as a man and as brave, not silly and stubborn as most women are."

So they were married. The poor old mother came to live in peace and plenty at the palace, and they all lived happily ever after, while the oldest daughter washed the dishes and the second daughter swept the floors. And if they haven't stopped, they are still washing and sweeping, for all I know.

Three Sisters

Once upon a time, a certain King had three daughters. Although they were sisters, they were very different from each other, so different that you never would have thought that they were sisters. They neither looked alike, nor did they like to do the same things. So they never played with each other.

The oldest one, tall and thin, spent most of her time reading old books and dreaming dreams of the stories she had read. She also liked to have her sisters wait on her and loved to give advice, telling them to do things she would never think of doing herself.

The second sister, short and plump, was so warm-hearted that she was always giving her things away, sometimes even things that didn't belong to her. She loved to make people happy by giving them presents.

The youngest sister was as strong as any boy, and she loved to run and jump and climb. She was always in such a hurry that she never looked where she was going and suffered many a bruise and bump. Nor did she look behind her to see what she had left behind, such things as muddy footprints, black finger marks, pieces of string, and scraps of paper. The servants spent a great deal of time putting the palace in order after she had whirled through it on her way out or in.

Now the King and his three daughters lived in a most beautiful palace built of clear, shining crystal. Lit by sunbeams during the day and by moonbeams at night, every room was filled with rich treasures: golden furniture, jeweled ornaments, silken draperies, and velvety carpets. The King had built this palace out of love for his daughters, hoping that they would grow to be as wise and good as the palace was beautiful.

When the time came for the old King to die, he called his three daughters to him and said, "All your life I have taken good care of you. And although you are as different from each other as the owl, the fish, and the horse, I have been able to keep you together, living as sisters, in our beautiful crystal palace. Now I am about to die, and you will be left alone. The palace and all its treasures will be yours to share and share alike. As long as you try to help each other to take good care of it, the palace will be yours. But let me warn you that if you don't, then you will have to go out into the world in search of a new home."

With these words, the old King died, and the three sisters were left to care for the palace and its treasures. Whereupon, the oldest sister told the others what they should do. She told the second sister to guard the palace treasures and the youngest to keep the house neat and clean. Then she went up to a room in one of the palace towers and settled down to read her books and dream her dreams. It did not occur to her to come down from her tower to see what her sisters were doing.

And what, indeed, were they doing? They also lived as they wished with no concern for anyone else. Little by little, the second sister gave away all the treasures to those who came begging. She gave away the golden dishes, the golden chairs, the golden tables, and every pretty thing that she found in the palace. Needless to say, this made all the beggars happy. Meanwhile, the youngest sister played freely everywhere, running and jumping and smashing things and tracking the walls and floors with dirty hands and feet.

Soon the shining crystal palace turned muddy and brown. The sunbeams and moonbeams could not shine in through the walls, so inside it grew to be as dark as a cave. And it was as empty as a cave too, for not only was all the furniture gone, but even the servants had left. No human being in his right mind wanted to stay in such an empty, dark house.

Now the three sisters had no one to cook for them, to wash or to bake, and it was not long before the oldest one came down from her tower to see why the chief butler had not brought her any food for three days. She found her two sisters quarreling in the bare and dingy throne room, blaming each other for what had happened.

"It's all your fault!" and "I didn't do anything!" they both shouted.

"I told you what to do," scolded the oldest. "Why didn't you do exactly as I said?"

"Oh, where shall we go now?" cried the youngest. "We can't stay here any longer or we will starve."

"Well," said the oldest, "I have been reading about the wide world and all the wonders to be seen there. We might as well go and look for a new home."

And so it happened, just as the old King had feared, for the three had not helped each other, and now they had to leave their old home in search of a new one.

This was not easy. They first had to travel over steep and rocky mountains. The two older sisters tired very quickly and stumbled and nearly fell from a high cliff. But they were saved by the youngest who ran fast enough to catch them and was strong enough to hold them and keep them from falling. Then she became their guide and helper and showed them just where to climb. She found the ledges where it was safest to step. She made tunnels for her sisters to crawl through the tangled undergrowth of bushes. She even jumped over the deepest chasms and made bridges of fallen trees over them so that her sisters could walk safely across. Were it not for her strength and courage, they all would have perished and never been heard of again. As it was, she helped them to cross the mountains safely, and at last they reached a low, open country and traveled on.

Now a second danger came upon them. A cold wind began to howl and moan across the plain. Rain, then hail and snow, fell from the heavens. The three sisters were at the mercy of the storm. Nowhere could they see a house or a tree, but only moors and meadows that offered no shelter. The oldest and the youngest thought they would die of cold, for the wind blew through their very bones, but they were helped by the plump sister who had enough fat on her bones to keep herself warm. She gave her big shawl to the oldest and her warm cloak to the youngest and so saved them from freezing to death.

Some days later, they entered into the midst of a dense forest, and here a third danger approached them, far worse than any other. Lost among the forest trees, they suddenly faced a wall of smoke and flame, for the forest was on fire. They ran ahead of it in fear and terror, but the wind blew the fire after them almost faster than they could run.

All at once the oldest sister cried, "Stop!"

"No, no!" the others answered, "The fire is coming so fast that it will soon overtake us."

"Stop and listen to me," said the oldest, "for I remember reading in a book that you can fight fire with fire. Now you do just what I tell you to do, and we can save ourselves."

For once, the other two were willing to follow their oldest sister's advice, and they did as they were told. The youngest ran quickly to the edge of the fire and seized a flaming branch and then flew back to the others as swiftly as the wind. Then they set fire to all the bushes and low branches that they could reach in a few minutes until they had made a wall of fire that rose up to meet the oncoming flames. The new fire stopped the old fire in its tracks, and the three sisters were saved.

Having now helped each other through such dangers, they reached a beautiful country of rolling hills and pleasant valleys. "Here," they thought, "we shall find our new home and live happily ever after." Little did they know what awaited them there.

This beautiful country was ruled by a dragon! And no sooner had the princesses set foot in the dragon's kingdom than the dragon himself charged down upon them, demanding that they become his slaves for a year and a day, or be eaten on the spot.

Needless to say, the three sisters wanted to live, so they went with the dragon to his cave, and there they stayed for many a day. The oldest sister kept the dragon entertained by telling him all the stories she had read. The second sister brought him gifts of flowers and fruits every day. The youngest one kept his cave neat and clean—so neat, so clean, that it shone almost as brightly as the beautiful crystal palace where they all had once lived.

A year passed and a day. On the evening of the last day, the dragon said to them, "You have served me well, and tomorrow you shall be free to go where you will."

But by this time, the three princesses had grown so fond of the dragon that they didn't want to leave him. In fact they wished for no other home. "Let us stay with you," they cried, "for we have no place to go!"

"Well, we shall see what we shall see," said the dragon. And as it was night, they all went to bed. When the sisters opened their eyes the next morning, they didn't know where they were. Instead of the gloom of the dragon's cave, the sun was shining so brightly that it made their eyes ache. Then as they grew used to the bright light and were able to see what surrounded them, they all cried out with amazement, for they found that they were in a beautiful crystal palace. The walls were so clean and clear that the whole palace was flooded with sunbeams. The floors were shining and spotless. The rooms were filled with beautiful treasures. It was all as it used to be when their father, the King, had lived.

They hurried down to the throne room to see if they might find him there, and whom should they see, seated on the throne, but a handsome, young prince who smiled when he saw them and called them to his side.

"I was the dragon, and you have set me free from the spell that bound me," said the Prince, and then he asked them if they would all stay with him and help him rule his kingdom. And of course they did.

But why had the Prince been turned into a dragon? Well, that would be the beginning of another story.

The Fir Tree

One winter day, some shepherds were guarding their sheep in the high mountains. Far above them towered the snow-covered peaks. For several days, they had grazed their sheep in a sheltered valley, and now all the grass was used up. So they decided to move on, over the snowy heights, in search of another green valley.

The oldest shepherd gave a call, and from all sides the sheep came running, while the dogs drove them all together, rounding up the few who didn't heed the shepherd's call right away. Then the shepherds headed the bellwether toward the mountains, and they all set out.

Timothy, the youngest shepherd, ran ahead of them all to find the safest paths. The sun was shining brightly, but the air got colder and colder as they climbed the steep slopes. When they reached the snow, Timothy had to be very careful to feel for solid ground under the snow and to find a way that didn't go near any deep crevasses into which the sheep might fall. Timothy had done this many times before and knew how. He was a brave boy. He was not afraid of wolves and had killed many to save his sheep. He was not afraid of snakes that hid in the grass to bite the sheep as they grazed; he had killed many snakes. Nor was he afraid of storms.

He looked up at the sky and saw a small cloud in the north. It didn't look like a storm cloud, but there it was! As they climbed ever higher into the mountains, the cloud got nearer and bigger. All the shepherds kept looking at it, but they said nothing. In their hearts, they hoped that they would find a sheltered valley before the snowstorm came.

All worked hard to travel fast—the men, the dogs, and the sheep. But they had to climb over a very high ridge, and the way was so steep that they could not go very fast. Soon the sky was almost covered by the dark cloud. The shepherds talked to their sheep, telling them to hurry on. The sheep struggled ahead and even stopped their bleating and climbed almost silently, as if for dear life.

Timothy was a good pathfinder. Just as the sky became quite black and the first flakes of snow began to fall, the whole company found themselves at the top of the ridge. Down on the other side appeared another valley where the grass showed green.

The snow was falling now quite thickly, and the shepherds paused to count their flock as the dogs raced around the sheep to drive them all together. Were they all safe? One little lamb began to bleat. They looked to see that he was calling for his mother. Where was she? She was the only one who was missing; yet she had been with them when they started.

The snowstorm was rapidly getting worse, but a shepherd will risk his life to save one of his sheep. "Take the flock to the valley below," said Timothy, "and I will search for the mother who is lost." Then he picked up the little, motherless lamb to carry it with him. Perhaps she would hear its bleating and answer.

So the other shepherds drove their flock below to the sheltered valley. Soon all were safe from wind and snow except Timothy and his lamb who went back the way they had come, in the face of the storm, to look for the mother sheep.

It was nearly night. The snow fell so thickly that Timothy could hardly see anything ahead of him. He carried the lamb inside his cape, and they kept each other warm. The wind blew more fiercely, and the snow turned to sleet and cut into Timothy's face. He pulled his woolly cap down over his eyes and ears and felt his way down the mountain with his feet and with his shepherd's crook held out before him.

"Cry, little one, for your mother, and maybe she will hear you," he said. And the little lamb bleated, "Maa– Maa–." And then Timothy gave the shepherd's call for lost sheep, but no sheep answered.

Down they went, step by step, calling and bleating, unable to see for the blackness of the night and the fierce and icy storm. It took them all night to reach the valley from which they had come the day before.

In the gray, early-morning light, Timothy saw that the meadow was covered with snow. Not a sheep track was to be seen. Perhaps the mother was buried in a drift! He spent the whole morning searching and calling, and the lamb was bleating and bleating, for he was hungry and homesick for his mother. But no mother did they find.

The snow had not stopped falling, and in the early afternoon, Timothy decided to go back up the mountain to try to join the other shepherds before dark. He was so tired that he could hardly lift his feet out of the deep snow. He wanted to go to sleep, but he knew that if he did, he would be covered with snow and never wake up again.

As he climbed upward, the storm seemed to get worse. The wind howled and beat him back with every step he took. The poor, hungry little lamb under his cape seemed to grow heavier and heavier. It was night again before he knew it. He struggled on until he could not take another step. Without wanting to, he fell down in a snow bank and went right to sleep, with the little lamb next to his heart still wrapped in his cape.

Then he dreamed that he was the lost mother-sheep lying at the bottom of a high cliff from which she had fallen. On all sides rose steep rocks that she could not climb, and there she lay calling and calling for the shepherd to come and find her. Suddenly she saw a beautiful light, and in the midst of the light stood a gentle and strong shepherd who had come to find her. So bright was the light that was shining in this dream that Timothy opened his eyes and woke up.

He saw that the storm was over. The stars shone in the clear sky overhead, and below on earth, the pure snow shone bright in the starlight. He saw one star brighter than all the rest, brighter than any he had ever seen before, and strangely enough, it shed its light in a shining pathway down to earth. The star seemed to be shining down on a special place somewhere nearby.

Timothy jumped up, and the lamb cried out for his mother. All that Timothy could think of was to find the place toward which the starlight was reaching. He hurried through the snowdrifts, no longer tired and hungry. He climbed over icy rocks, hooked his shepherd's crook around tree trunks and pulled himself up the steep slopes, ever toward the rays of the gleaming star.

Suddenly he stood on a high place and looked down into another snow-covered valley where the path of starlight touched the earth, and right in the midst of the light stood a single fir tree. All around this spot, the valley was dark, but there the star's light was bright.

Down Timothy went toward the starlit fir tree. Nearer and nearer he came. The little lamb began to bleat again, as if to say, "Hurry, hurry, hurry." And then they reached the fir tree.

It was filled with light. Its long branches sloped down like a snug roof, and there under the shelter of the branches, where the light was brightest, stood the mother sheep, safe and well and nibbling some grass that grew green under the thick fir branches.

The little lamb was so happy to find his mother. He frisked and played, and she gave him milk and he ate some grass and felt strong and hearty again. Even Timothy felt fresh and strong and as happy as the lamb in finding his lost sheep.

As the sun rose over the mountains, Timothy led the mother sheep and her lamb away from the sheltering fir tree. Before the day was over, they found the other shepherds and the flock.

When Timothy told his friends all that had happened to him, they said, "It was a sign from Heaven that something wonderful is going to happen."

The Lazy Gnome

Once there was a little Gnome who didn't like to work. Now this was very strange, for most gnomes are never so happy as when they are busy with their shovels and pick axes, digging in the earth. In the autumn, they make earth beds for the little Seed Children to sleep in. In the winter, they search for treasures of gold and silver and precious stones for the Gnome King. In the spring and summer, they dig the ground to make it loose and airy to let in sun warmth and rainwater so that the Seed Children can breathe and drink and grow up toward the sun.

Although most gnomes like their work, this one was lazy and went to so much trouble to get out of work that it took up all his time. He would hide from the others among the deep-growing roots of trees. If they found him, he would pretend to be helping the Seed Children, or to be looking for diamonds and rubies. He never lifted a shovel or a pick-axe if he could help it. But if he had to, he would lay it down as soon as no one was looking, and there he would just sit and do nothing.

One day, the Gnome King came upon him as he sat doing nothing. "What kind of a gnome are you?" the King shouted, in a rage. "Why are you not about your business? This is the time of year when the search for treasure is going on. Don't you see how busily your brothers are working?"

"Sire," answered the Gnome, "I was just getting ready to start work."

"Where are your shovel and pick-axe?" asked the King.

"I lost them in a deep hole, which I had dug in search of jewels."

"Where is the hole?"

"Far from here, Your Majesty, so far that I cannot find my way to it again."

"You're a humbug!" shouted the Gnome King. "We've no use for humbugs in this kingdom. You are herewith ordered to leave my kingdom, and don't come back unless you can bring me twelve diamonds every day."

So the lazy Gnome had to go away. He could not stay with his fellows underground. Up he went to the surface of the earth and found a hollow tree into which he crawled and went to sleep.

When he woke up, spring had come, and he looked out of the hole in the tree to see all around him a green meadow. The most beautiful colors filled the meadow—pink and yellow and violet and blue and orange! These were the meadow flowers. And in and out and among the flowers flew the golden Sun Fairies, bringing sunbeams to each flower to help it bloom. They were singing as they flew about. Sometimes they joined hands and flew in a happy circle around a flower. Oh, what a good time they were having—singing, dancing, swooping, flying—and they were so beautiful that the Gnome longed to play with them and be one of them

"Let me play with you," he called to a circle of happy Sun Fairies. "Let me play too!"

"We are not playing," they laughed. "We are at work. Our work is to help the flowers bloom in the meadow. When they bloom well, we are very happy!" Then they all flew up toward the sun to gather more sunbeams.

"Well," thought the lazy Gnome, "they are fools to be so happy while they work. How could work be so much fun?" And when he thought of his brothers down under the ground digging the air and water tunnels for the Seed Children, he was glad not to be there.

The Gnome crawled out of his hollow tree and crossed the meadow until he came to a beautiful, blue stream of water. As it flowed along, it came to a rocky ledge over which it tumbled and turned into a gleaming white waterfall. There, in the white, shining spray, the Gnome saw some Water Fairies who were rising and sinking as if to enjoy the falling water. They, too, were singing and laughing with joy as they tossed sprays of water drops up into the air. *What fun it would be to splash in the waterfall with them!* thought the Gnome. "Let me play with you," he called to them.

They heard him and laughed and answered, "We are not playing. We are at work. Our work is to send the water up into the sky until there is enough to make a big, dark rain cloud. Then the rain will fall to help the Plant Children grow." Then with a shout of joy, they flashed down the stream to find another place to work, leaving the lazy Gnome all alone.

Can it really be such fun to work so hard? he thought to himself. "I wish I could find something that would be fun to do."

Now the sun set and the blue sky grew bluer and bluer and darker and darker 'til at last it was quite dark. What a strange feeling he had! He was all alone and so far from home. He began to be homesick, but he knew that if he went back to the gnome kingdom, he'd have to take a pick-axe and work for the Gnome King. Never, never! Yet it would be nice to have at least one companion.

As he looked up in the sky, he saw something bright—a light, very high, twinkling and sparkling, oh, so far up. Soon another appeared, then many more until the whole sky was shining with stars of light. While watching, the Gnome saw a cloud of swift fairies flying like the wind, all covered with shimmering light and carrying in their hands heaps more of what seemed like silver dust. They were in a great hurry, but they were making beautiful patterns of light in the air.

As the fairies flew over the ground near him, he heard a sweet humming like the sound of wind blowing among trees. The fairies were humming as they flew, and their faces wore smiles of joy.

"Where are you going?" cried the Gnome. "Do let me come with you."

"That you cannot do," they answered, "for we are beings of the air, and you are an earth gnome."

"Just let me play with you, then," he begged.

"Oh, we have no time to play. Before the sun rises again, we must carry stardust to every part of the world. No one on earth would ever wake up happy and gay if we did not scatter stardust every night." And so they flew on, faster than ever to get their work done.

"No one has any time for me!" complained the Gnome crossly, and he did not know where to go or what to do. Wondrously, he did not feel like just sitting and doing nothing. So he stumbled along without looking where he was going and fell into a deep hole in the ground. At the bottom of the hole, he sat up and looked around and listened. Nearby he heard some sounds: "Tick-tack, tick-tack, tkk." Ah! He knew the way those pick-axes sounded, digging the earth loose. Then he heard some jolly voices singing,

>Hi-yo, Hi-yo!
>We dig the earth so dry-o
>To help the baby seeds grow
>Till they reach the sky-o.
>Hi-yo, Hi-yo!

"They're hard at it!" muttered the lazy Gnome. "They sound happy too, just like all the others, the Sun Fairies, the Water Fairies, and the ones who fly in the wind and starlight." Then he thought, *If we didn't do our work down here underground, the others wouldn't find anything to take care of up there.*

Before he knew it, he was hurrying toward the sound of the pick-axes, and the next thing that happened was very unexpected. The lazy Gnome stepped in beside all the working gnomes, and grasping a pick-axe, he began to swing it and sing,

>Hi-yo, Hi-yo!
>We dig the earth so dry-o
>To help the baby seeds grow
>Till they reach the sky-o.
>Hi-yo, Hi-yo!

And after that, he was never lazy again.

The Lazy Water Fairy

One spring day as the Water Fairies were sporting in a clear mountain brook, a troop of Air Fairies flew over the water calling to the Water Fairies to leave their brook, to come with them to a far-away garden where the Gnomes wanted some help. "For," said the Air Fairies, "the Fire Fairies have dried up the ground, and the Bulb and Seed Children are thirsty, and the Gnomes cannot help them to grow unless you bring them some water."

Then with a glad shout, the Water Fairies took hands with the Air Fairies, and they flew off together to help the Gnomes.

There was one little Water Fairy who didn't go. She was floating on her back in the brook, enjoying herself, and she didn't want to work. No, she much preferred just floating on her back and watching the blue sky, the birds fly, the bees buzz, and the butterflies flutter. She was left alone in the brook while all her friends were far away helping the Plant Children.

The brook carried her along down the mountainside until it reached a waterfall. There in the waterfall was another band of Water Fairies who were working hard to splash the spray of the waterfall over the ground at each side of the stream so that the trees and wild flowers would have something to drink. Although they called to her, our lazy Water Fairy did not join them. She slid over the waterfall and slipped down into the pool beneath it, still amusing herself by watching the blue sky, the birds fly, the bees buzz, and the butterflies flutter among the flowers.

A wider stream flowed out from the pool, and she floated into this and let it carry her for many long miles until it entered a wide river. There she met with another large band of Water Fairies who called to her, "Come with us and help us carry water to the fields for the corn and the wheat." Then they rushed off along a little side river that flowed in the direction of some wide fields.

But the lazy Water Fairy did not go with them. She lay on her back in the wide river enjoying herself as she watched the blue sky, the birds fly, the bees buzz, and the butterflies flutter.

The big river bore many boats that were journeying toward the sea. On its banks were towns and villages, and children came to the shore to fish and play. There was so much to watch that the Water Fairy was very happy.

Floating down the broad river, which grew broader and broader, the lazy one traveled far without even trying. At last, she heard a great sound of waves dashing against a shore, and there the river let itself go and flowed out into the great ocean.

The waves of the ocean were wild and high, and the lazy Water Fairy couldn't lie on her back and watch the sky anymore. No, it was too rough and lively, so she let herself sink down and down, deep into the undersea where she could drift very comfortably and watch all the fishes and sea creatures—sunfish, starfish, sea snakes, seahorses, sharks, whales, and many more—all hunting for food.

At last she came to a beautiful, pink coral sea palace and drifted lazily through the arched, open windows into a room where sat a Sea Princess surrounded by crowds and crowds of Water Fairies. Among them were all the friends of the lazy one from the mountain brook.

The Sea Princess was a beautiful mermaid with flowing, blue hair. She had eyes as blue as the sea, cheeks as pink as coral, and hands as white as the sea foam. Her home was in the sea, and as she could never leave it, all the Water Fairies were telling her of the wonders that they had seen and the work they had done. They told her how exciting it was to ride in the sky on the shoulders of the Wind Giants who blew the storms over the land as the lightning flashed and the thunder crashed, and how they then poured down from the clouds bringing rain to the dry earth. Then the Sea Princess kissed them all and said, "You have done very well, for the poor earth would die without your help."

They told her how busy they had been under the ground working with the Gnomes to help the plants grow, how they had carried streams of trickling water through the little tunnels the Gnomes had dug to the thirsty roots of the plants. Then the Sea Princess gave them each a little hug and said, "You have done very well, for the poor plants would die without your help."

They told her how they had filled all the wells on earth with fresh, clear water so that the human beings could have plenty to drink and could wash everything clean. Then the Sea Princess gave them each a shining pearl and said, "You have done very well, for without your help the poor human beings could not live."

All the Water Fairies sang joyfully, and after kissing the Sea Princess goodbye, they hurried away up to the surface of the ocean where their friends, the Air Fairies, were waiting to take them up to the clouds and over the land. Early every morning, many of them descended to earth carrying their sea pearls that became dewdrops for the flowers and grasses to drink. Others, gathered in the big wet clouds, poured rain upon the earth, each one riding down in a big, wet raindrop.

In the meantime, the lazy Water Fairy, who had heard the other Water Fairies talking to the Sea Princess, lay on her back on the floor of the sea and waited for something else to happen. But it was all very still down there because it was so deep, and so she went to sleep.

She slept a long time. While she was sleeping, strange things happened. First, she became covered with the green sea slime that settles on all under the sea that doesn't move. Then white sea sand settled on the green sea slime and stuck to it and made a hard shell around the Water Fairy. When at last she woke up, she found herself caught in a hard shell prison without a single window through which she might look.

Now the Water Fairy could really be lazy, and there she is to this day in a prison, apart from all her friends who are free and happy as they journey through earth and sky and sea, always bringing help to the life on earth.

The Four Seasons

Father Sun looked down from his shining throne in the blue heaven and saw that there were four brothers battling with each other for the right to rule the earth.

First came the oldest brother from his cold ice palace in the northern skies. He rode a snow-white horse and carried an icy spear. His robes were made of swirling snow. His beard was white with glistening icicles. His eyes were black and cold. Around and about him the North Wind danced and whistled and shrieked, "Make way for the King, the ruler of the whole world."

Wherever this great, cold brother went, the earth became covered with snow. The brooks and rivers turned into ice, the rabbits and squirrels and mice and bears all hid themselves in holes and went to sleep. The birds flew as fast as they could toward the south to get away from the cold, and human beings looked out of the windows of their houses and shivered.

When he had spread his snow and ice far and wide, the Ice King was happy and built himself a new ice palace in the midst of his snowfields wherein he rested and slept. He and the whole earth might have slept forever except there came a wind from the west, blowing over the snow.

The West Wind was warm and filled with drops of rain. He was the messenger of the Ice King's youngest brother who now came forth from his palace in the western skies to win the world for himself.

Wearing a suit of pale green, a wreath of new green leaves in his hair, and breathing his warm breath, over the snowy hills he came. The raindrops melted the snow, and it disappeared as he passed. In the brooks and rivers, the ice cracked and melted, and the raindrops began to sing and jump and splash and dash on toward the sea. The earth grew soft and warm. New buds bloomed on trees. Birds flew back from the south to build their nests. The rabbits and squirrels and mice and bears woke up and came out of their holes. The human beings started to plow their fields, dig their gardens, and plant their seeds.

The Ice King woke up and sent a great army of snow and hail to fight his youngest brother. But the youngest brother fought with warm raindrops that conquered the snow and hail and turned them into rain and mist, and the defeated Ice King fled away to the north.

So for a while, the earth was alive with sprouting seeds and buds, with tender shoots and new green leaves. Baby birds hatched out of their eggs. Baby kittens were born in the barns, as well as puppies and chicks, and the woods were full of baby animals all newborn and growing. Before all the young plants and animals had even grown up, however, there came from the south a new army to fight for the earth's riches.

This was the army of the third brother who was from the southern skies, whose breath was as hot as fire, whose robes of shining yellow blazed as warmly as the Sun's rays. His hair was as bright as the Sun. His eyes were as blue as the sky. His helper was the hot South Wind who commanded all the hot breezes of the south as they shot little flames over the earth, burning and scorching whatever they touched.

A long battle was fought between the two brothers, the hot one and the one whose gentle warmth had brought the plants and animals to life. For days and days the hot winds blew, and the brother from the west called forth his raindrop soldiers to fight the heat. Sometimes it seemed as if the hot one were winning, for many brooks and rivers dried up, leaves turned brown, flowers wilted, animals were thirsty, and human beings saw their fields and gardens wither in the heat. Then would come the raindrop army, and for a while the hot winds would disappear, later to return in greater fury.

However, while this battle raged, it brought about good deeds on earth, for the fruits that formed in the flowers drank of the raindrops that fell into the soil, and the hot winds blew upon them so they became warm and ripe and juicy. Berries ripened for the birds, carrots for the rabbits, nuts for the squirrels, and wheat and corn for the human beings. All beings on earth were happy so long as the battle continued, but the two brothers were not happy, for neither one could conquer the other.

Then the fourth brother came growling out of the eastern skies. His eyes were gray and cool. His cloak was orange and brown. In his armies were cold winds and frost fairies. His general was the biting East Wind. As the fourth brother prowled over the earth, his chill winds chased the hot south winds away, his frost soldiers turned the warm raindrops to sleet. Leaves and fruits and seed pods all turned brown and orange and fell from the trees and bushes to the ground. All the little animals burrowed into their holes to keep warm. The birds flew south, leaving the bare trees and their empty nests behind them. The ponds became frosty, the grasses turned brown, and the whole earth seemed cold and sad.

Now the North Wind came back leading the way for his master from the north, dancing and shrieking, "Make way for the King, the ruler of the whole world!"

So came the great cold brother once more, with his freezing breath and his hosts of snowy soldiers. They came in the night and surprised the one who had come from the east. They drove him away, covered the fields and gardens with snow, froze the frosty ponds to solid ice, and put the world to sleep.

Year followed year as the four brothers fought each other for the sake of ruling the earth, but not one of them ever won. At last they agreed among themselves: "No one of us can win the earth. Let us ask the great Sun, the Father of Life on earth, to appoint one of us to be King. That will settle it and we can stop our fighting."

Whereupon, they called upon the Father Sun to settle their dispute, for they were tired of fighting. The Sun had, for many years, been watching their battles, and he had seen how each brother brought certain good things to the earth. And so the Sun spoke thus to the four brothers:

"No one of you should rule the earth, but rather each of you in turn, for you each bring good to the earth if you don't stay too long. Let each one rule in his season and then give place to another, in this order: The one who awakens the earth with his warm breath so that all the plants and animals spring to life, let him be called Spring. Let Spring do his work. Then let the hot one from the southern skies come to ripen all fruits and berries and grains. Let him be called Summer. Let Summer do his work, which ends when the seeds have fanned in the fruits. Then let the cool one from the east send forth his East Wind to blow the seeds to earth. And let him be called Fall, for in his time all leaves and seeds shall fall to the earth. Then let the cold one from the north take up his task and freeze the earth in a deep sleep and cover it with blankets of snow. Let him be called Winter. Let Winter rule the time of rest until Spring awakens the beings of earth again."

And so it happens that even today Spring, Summer, Fall, and Winter share in ruling the earth, that the earth may work and rest, wake and sleep, according to the seasons.

The Rainbow

Great King Sun, who lights the world, has many messengers and servants to carry out his wishes upon the earth. Among these is the Wind, a great being who can encircle the seven seas as well as all the lands with his breath. Then there are the Sun Fairies, whose spears bring the Sun's light down to earth, and the Rain Fairies, who gather drops of mist from the clouds and turn them into raindrops that water the earth.

To these tiny Sun Fairies and Rain Fairies, the great King Sun gave the special task of caring for the Plant Children on earth. Because of this, the Sun and Rain Fairies loved all the little Plant Children and tried to win their favor! But once ...

Once there was a wee, shining, golden Sun Fairy who was very young and thought that he knew a very great deal. When he was flying about one day, he bumped into a Rain Fairy who was blue and cold and who had fallen out of a cloud.

"How blue and cross you look, you poor miserable little rain bringer!" the Sun Fairy teased.

"Miserable indeed!" responded the Rain Fairy." You're not as bright as you think you are. Why, without us, who bring rain to earth, the little Plant Children could not grow."

"As if the Plant Children needed you!" said the Sun Fairy scornfully. "We Sun Fairies with our spears of light are the ones who help the Plant Children to grow."

"No, no!" cried the Rain Fairy. "We are the ones who help them."

"You are not!" shouted the Sun Fairy. "We are."

"No, we are!" The Rain Fairy began to swell with rage and to look like a blue bubble.

"We are!" roared the Sun Fairy. He turned, red with anger, and his spear began to look like a red-hot flame.

They made such a hullabaloo that all the other fairies came rushing to the spot to see what was going on. Thousands and millions of light-bearing Sun Fairies swarmed toward thousands and millions of Rain Fairies who poured down from some drifting clouds.

The young Sun Fairy shouted to his bright brothers, "Come, gather and listen. The Rain Fairies think they are the ones who help the Plant Children grow!" And all the Sun Fairies flashed their golden spears with rage, and the spears glowed red with anger, like flames of fire.

"Oooh!" cried the blue Rain Fairy to his dark brothers. "The Sun Fairies say they are the ones who help the Plant Children grow."

Now when great King Sun heard their quarreling, he laughed, for he knew better, and he sighed, for he feared they would not believe him if he told them the truth. So he decided to let them fight it out and find out for themselves. Summoning the Wind, he commanded, "Go and blow the Rain Fairies away so the Sun Fairies will learn a good lesson."

Then a great windstorm arose in the sky as the Wind blew the clouds away, and for many days thereafter not a cloud appeared in the clear, blue sky.

Day after day the Sun Fairies flew among the Plant Children, showering them with sunshine. The days grew warmer and warmer, and the Plant Children began to get thirsty.

"We are so thirsty," they cried. "We want a drink of water." But the Sun Fairies pretended not to hear.

Then the ground became hotter and hotter, and the Plant Children cried, "We are burning up!" And their little green coats began to scorch and turn brown. Still, the Sun Fairies paid no attention to their cries.

Then all the brooks and rivers dried up and there was no water anywhere. The Plant Children turned black and curled up and died, all except the great Trees who were stronger than the rest. When they saw what had happened, they complained to their friend, the Wind.

"Oh, Wind," said they, "the Rain Fairies have not visited us for so long that our little ones have died of thirst. Blow north, south, east, and west, oh Wind, until you find where the Rain Fairies are hiding, and tell them to bring us rain."

So the Wind hurried away and found the Rain Fairies all hiding in a great cloud above a high mountain. And he told them to hurry down with rain to help the Plant Children come to life again.

Then the Wind blew many great rain clouds down over the earth, and the Rain Fairies leaped from the clouds, splashing great showers of rain over the earth and shouting at the Sun Fairies, who fled at their coming, "You have killed the Plant Children with your red and yellow fire. We are the ones who really give them life."

High in the sky, above the Clouds, great King Sun watched what was happening. He smiled to himself and sighed and decided that the Rain Fairies should have their turn and learn their lesson.

Day after day it rained. The rain made the earth wet again, and baby plants started to grow. Soon all the old, black and brown and dead Plant Children were hidden by new, green baby plants, and they grew well for a time. The Rain Fairies were very busy, making sure that it didn't stop raining. After a while, the ground got too wet and turned into mud.

The newly-grown Plant Children cried, "We are too cold and wet!"

Now the Rain Fairies pretended not to hear them. Then the earth got so watery that it began to slide away in little streams of muddy water, leaving the Plant Children with no covering for their roots.

Again the Plant Children cried, "Our feet are slipping. We will drown in all this water!" Even then, the Rain Fairies paid no attention.

Then the brooks and rivers filled up so full with rainwater that they overflowed their banks, and the water spread out in all directions, flooding the land and drowning all the baby plants. Again the big Trees saw what was happening and complained to their friend, the Wind.

"Oh, Wind, the Rain Fairies bring too much rain, for they have flooded the land and our babies are drowning. Blow the Rain Fairies away and call the Sun Fairies back for a while to dry up the water."

So the Wind blew and blew, and as the clouds scattered, the Rain Fairies saw that they had drowned all the little Plant Children, and they were very much ashamed.

Now, as the Rain Fairies were flying away, they happened to meet the Sun Fairies coming back, and this time both Rain Fairies and Sun Fairies knew better than to boast and fight. And so they stopped to greet each other in the sky, singing, "The Plant Children need us both. Not too much sunshine, and not too much of rain, but both rain and sunshine will make them grow again."

When great King Sun heard this, he smiled again, and this time he did not sigh, for he knew that all was well. Indeed, the Sun Fairies and the Rain Fairies decided to make peace with each other and each do their share to help the Plant Children grow. To celebrate their new friendship, they danced together in a great arch in the sky, and then something wonderful happened.

As the red Sun Fairies danced with the blue Rain Fairies, the arch shone with a violet light, just the color of the little violets that grow among the plants on earth. And as the yellow Sun Fairies danced among the blue Rain Fairies, a lovely green light shone in the arch, just the green that the plants wear in their stems and leaves. And soon there shone in the arch all the colors of the plant family: violet, blue, green, yellow, orange, and red.

Working together, the Sun Fairies and Rain Fairies give their rainbow colors to the fruits of the earth: purple grapes, blue plums, green cabbages, yellow corn, orange pumpkins, and red apples. And they make them juicy and sweet. And when we see a rainbow in the sky, we know that the Sun Fairies and Rain Fairies are having a good time together.

The Prince of Butterflies

Dame Nature, who can be everywhere at once, can herself see everything at once, and so she knows all the secrets of the plants and the pebbles and the wee creatures that make up the earth. Sometimes she makes her appearance in a single place, the better to advise and forewarn those who do not have her wisdom.

Once upon a time, she took up her abode in a great, hollow tree. She put on a cloak as yellow as an autumn leaf and a bonnet as green as new grass, and sat by her door singing a song for all to hear:

> Ah! Oh!
> Wonder and woe!
> The sights that I see!
> The things that I know!

Among the many who heard her singing and who stopped to listen was a humble insect named Twig. Twig was a caterpillar who lived in constant fear of being eaten by the hungry birds that lived in the trees. As he listened to her song, he wondered if such a wise old dame could tell him what was to become of him.

"Good-day, Granny," said Twig, when the song was over.

"Good-day, good-day," said Dame Nature kindly. "What can I do for you, my child?"

"I am only a caterpillar," Twig said meekly, "but I would like to be happy. As it is, I am usually in such danger of being swallowed by a hungry bird that I can never enjoy myself. Even when there are no birds around, I am not very happy. My poor head is full of strange ideas. It seems I shall never be happy unless I can fly. It is all very sad, for of course I have no wings, and I don't know what is to become of me."

"And if you wish to fly, you shall," said Dame Nature with a gleam in her eye. "Be patient and never fear, for the time will come when you will fly through the air on golden wings, higher than any bird."

"How can that be possible?" whispered Twig, trembling with excitement. "How can it be?"

"Nevertheless, it is true," said she, nodding wisely. "But before you get ready to fly, you must learn an important secret. Once you have learned that secret, you will fall sound asleep, with many a dream to keep you happy. And when you awake, you will look at yourself to see that I was right."

"Can it be true? Can it be true?" cried Twig. "To think that I shall fly. How beautiful it will be."

As he went on his way, he wept with joy, "To think that I shall fly! How beautiful it will be! Who am I, to have golden wings?"

In a few days' time he was quite used to the idea, and he went to see all his friends. "It may surprise you to know that soon I shall be able to fly," he said to them mysteriously.

"Indeed!" said the ant. "In that case I must learn how to swim."

"One needs wings before one can fly, my poor Twig," said the beetle.

"That will be fine," said the spider, "but take care not to fly into my web!"

Their answers made Twig wish that he had not said anything. How could he expect them to believe him? When the time came, they could see for themselves, and until then, he would have to keep away from them.

So he went off by himself and tried to be patient, wondering what secret he would learn. But there was no one to tell him any secrets. Whenever he went to sleep, he dreamed that all the birds in the world were flapping around him, and he would wake up in a great fright only to see that he was as far from flying as ever.

"The old dame must have been wrong," he said mournfully. "I expect I shall spend the rest of my life crawling around without any wings, only to be swallowed by a hateful bird in the end."

As he wandered through the grass, he came face to face with his friend, the ant, who made fun of him, saying, "Still crawling about, I see!"

Twig did not answer. When the ant had gone, he wept in despair, and as there was no one to comfort him, he hurried back to find Dame Nature to see what she would say.

There she sat by the door of her hollow tree in her yellow cloak and green bonnet, singing,

Come what may,
Go what may,
Come and go what may.
I see the sights
And know the things
That happen far away!

When she had finished her song, she spoke to Twig, "Oh-ho," she said, "so you are back again! And you are feeling sad for no reason at all. That is a pity."

"I have a good reason to be sad," grumbled Twig. "All you said about secrets and dreams and golden wings hasn't helped me out of my troubles. No one has told me any secrets, and each time I go to sleep I have bad dreams that frighten me to death. So, in spite of what you said, I don't know what will become of me."

"You are an impatient creature," said the wise old dame in a stern voice. "It won't help you to grumble and fuss. Go home and keep your patience. When you are ready to fly, you will."

"If only I were sure!" wailed the caterpillar as he went home again. "I think it is harder to wait for things to happen than never to have them happen at all."

But once he made up his mind to be patient, time passed quite pleasantly. He became so used to waiting that he was almost happy.

And then one morning as he looked around him, everything seemed changed. Each blade of grass was dancing in the breeze. The flowers seemed very gay, nodding their heads and whispering among themselves, and there were no bird voices in the rustling trees overhead.

"What a lovely world this is!" said Twig very softly. "I may be a caterpillar of no importance, but in my heart I am flying higher than any bird, and that is all that matters."

Nature had said, "Before you fly, you must learn an important secret." Now he was sure he knew the secret.

Suddenly he felt very sleepy, so he wrapped himself snugly in a leaf and went right to sleep. In his dreams he chased the wind over the tops of the tallest trees and floated to earth in showers of sunbeams, only to rise with the wind again. He never knew how long he slept. His dreams were so sweet that even the cold snows of winter did not disturb him.

When, at last, he awoke to crawl out of his leaf blanket, he knew that he was still himself, and yet he felt like someone else. He had fewer legs and they felt very weak. As he rested in the warm, spring sunshine, they grew stronger and he stood up. Then he discovered that he was wearing a close-fitting cloak. As it slowly spread out around him, he trembled with joy.

"How beautiful they are, how beautiful!" he whispered, fluttering his wings slowly up and down while a sunbeam sprinkled them with gold. Each moment they grew stronger, until finally they lifted him away from the ground high into the air.

He flew about very carefully so as to get used to them and then went straight to the hollow tree in search of his well-remembered friend, Dame Nature. And there she was, on her doorstep, singing one of her songs:

> Yesterday was,
> Tomorrow will be,
> But they're one and the same to me.
> The dreams of kings
> And of smaller things
> Are plain for me to see.

"Good-day, Granny," he said when she had finished her song.

"Good-day, good-day," she answered. "And what can I do for you, my child?"

"I have come to show you my wings," he said, fluttering them gracefully before her. They are such beautiful wings, but a bit hard to manage as yet."

"So I see," said Dame Nature with a twinkle in her eye, "and poor Twig with all his troubles is now the Prince of Butterflies!"

The Snowflake

(adapted from "Snow" by Marcia Dodwell)

Clear, glistening Little Drop of Water was rushing and playing and racing down the hill with all his brothers to the sea. A great wave rose and caught them all and threw them into the air so fast that they all shouted and laughed with joy. High in the air, Little Drop of Water hung for a moment but didn't have time to fall back into the sea, for three bright Sun Fairies fanned him with their wings, and up – up – up he rose, so far and so high that he was soon in the sky, way above the highest mountain.

It was cold up there, so cold that Little Drop of Water froze. He couldn't run and spill any more! He tried to go down and up, forward and backward, right and left, and each time he moved in each direction, he froze in that direction until he was like a tiny, six-pointed star.

All around him, his many brothers likewise had become six-pointed stars, just like him and yet not like him, for every single one was formed in a different pattern. They all admired each other so much that they couldn't decide which one was the most beautiful. And what's more, they could float in the air like feathers. Here and there—wherever Wind blew them—they floated.

They let the Wind carry them a long way, until they bumped into Big Old Mountain, who refused to get out of the way. If the Wind wanted to get by him, he would have to blow either around him or over him. Nor did Big Old Mountain ever say, "Excuse me." So with a shriek and a whistle, the Wind blew up one side and down the other. In passing, he left all the beautiful, six-pointed Snowflakes on the top of the Mountain, who suddenly looked like an old, old giant with snow-white hair.

There the Snowflakes lay and rested for many days, but at last they wished they could be on their way. They knew they didn't want to stay there forever. Sure enough, the Sun rose earlier one morning and said, "The days are going to be longer now for a while, and my child the Earth is going to be warmed and comforted."

As the Sun's warmth covered the Snowflakes, they suddenly slipped down from the mountaintop. They began to run and roll and, in a twinkling, they turned into drops of water again. All together they poured down the side of Big Old Mountain in a pure, sweet stream of water, laughing and gurgling with joy and gladness. Those who could listen heard the voice of the water singing: "Gloria, Gloria."

Now, what do you suppose Little Drop of Water, who had been a Snowflake, did next? He slipped under ground until he was out of sight. There, under the Earth, an old, old Gnome picked him up and carried him to a little Seedling who was thirsty.

"Drink," said the old Gnome to the Seedling. "This pure, clear Little Drop of Water will help you to grow."

"I will carry him up to the beautiful Sun," answered Little Wheat Sprout.

So Little Drop of Water entered into the plant and slowly, slowly rose up in her as she grew taller and taller. At last he entered into a tiny grain of the wheat that formed at the end of her stalk—up in the sunshine above the ground. He felt very proud and noble because the plant had wrapped him around with a beautiful, green jacket, and as the Sun shone down on him, the green turned to a glorious gold, the very color of the Sun itself.

One day, the harvesters came to harvest the wheat. All the Wheat in the field was filled with joy now that the time had come for it to be made into bread, which would bring life and strength to human beings. And in each grain of wheat, bearing the pureness and goodness of Heaven from which they came, many Little Drops of Water lay waiting to enter into the bread.

So the Wheat was harvested and threshed, and the crystal-clear grains were taken to a city called Bethlehem, which means the House of Bread. There in a stable, a little child—the Christ Child who had also come down from Heaven—welcomed the bread in which the Snowflakes were hidden, and it became the Bread of Life.

And even today, little "snowflake water drops," hiding in the golden loaves, are filled with joy, for the Bread of Life nourishes each little child who comes into the world.

Four Words

One spring day, a little Gnome woke up a little Seed Child, who was sleeping soundly underground. "Wake up, wake up!" cried the Gnome.

Still half asleep, the little Seed Child answered, "Oh, oh—it is so long since I fell asleep that it's hard to remember who I am. Please, kind Gnome, tell me my name."

"I remember your name," answered the Gnome, "for I have to remember the names of all the Seed Children. Last autumn you gave me your name to keep for you, and now you may have it back. It is Violet."

As soon as she heard her name, little Violet felt happy and wanted to really wake up and do something. "Now what shall I do?" she asked.

"My friend, the Water Fairy, will tell you," answered the Gnome.

So he called to the Water Fairy, who spoke to little Violet and said, "You must grow!"

As soon as Violet heard the word "grow," she pushed her little head up, and stretched her little feet down, and pushed and stretched, while the Gnome danced around singing her name, and the Water Fairy brought her many cool drinks of water, saying, "Grow, grow, grow."

As soon as Violet's little head peeped above the ground into the air, an Air Fairy greeted her, saying, "Fast, fast, fast!" Then her short, green stems grew tall, her tiny, green leaves grew broad, and her little head grew larger and larger.

At last one day, a Sun Fairy touched her head with his wand of light, saying, "I bring you a color from the rainbow, and it is purple."

Violet felt so happy that she lifted her head high and let forth her beautiful, purple petals. Now the Gnome, the Water Fairy, the Air Fairy, and the Sun Fairy all sang to greet her with the words each one had given her:

"Purple violet, grow fast."

The Boy and the Tree

"How do plants grow?" the children asked their grandmother.

"The sun," said she. "But did you know that the sun also helps you to grow?" Then she told them a story.

Once upon a time, there was a little baby. On the day he was born, his father planted a baby oak tree beside the house. The father thought that as his son grew, so would the oak grow and be his son's tree—to give him shade while he lived and to mark the place of his birth even after he died.

Both the boy and the tree grew well, but of course they were always very different from each other. The boy's father and mother, who helped each to grow, often wished their son would be as quiet as his companion, the young oak tree.

When the boy and the tree were two years old, the boy was running everywhere—in and out of the house, under people's feet, taking things off the shelves, putting them in his mouth, picking the green tomatoes, pulling up the young plants in the garden, and breaking his toys and his mother's teacups. He had to be watched every minute. But the oak tree grew without having to be watched every minute.

Then the boy grew bigger. He learned not to reach for everything and what was good to eat and what was not, but he also learned how to say, "No!" and "I don't want to!" and to do just the opposite of what his mother or father asked him to do. That was part of his growing, not at all like the tree whose roots became stronger and whose branches spread out to give a little shade, just as people wanted it to.

The tree's spreading hands were not like the boy's hands, for as the boy grew older, his hands were quick to snatch toys away from his brothers and sisters and to hold onto them. Many a time now, the boy showed that he was learning to look out for himself, saying, "I want it!" or "It's mine!" He got into many scraps and squabbles because he felt strong and brave. He shouted a lot and pushed other children down and blamed them for being the ones to "start it."

Although his father and mother loved their boy dearly, they often looked at each other and sighed, "How peacefully and steadily the oak tree grows. It is even taller than our son!"

So it happened that the tree outgrew the boy until its top was higher than the roof on their house. But as you have seen, a tree's growing is very different from a child's. While the tree is putting out new roots, new branches, new leaves, and pushing its way up toward the sun, the child is learning to run and to reach. While the tree is obeying the will of the Sun and the Earth and the Rain and all that helps it grow, the boy is disobeying all those who want to help him grow. And while the tree is giving its shade to all who ask for it, the boy is snatching toys from other children or pushing them out of his way.

The tree became tall and green and shady, a blessing to the people of the house. And the boy kept on growing too. He didn't grow as tall as the tree, but one day he stopped snatching and pushing. He had learned something new. It had grown inside him just as the oak tree's shade-giving leaves had grown outside it. His father and mother noticed it the first time he made his bed without being told. They noticed it again when he offered to carry his mother's market basket for her, and again when he kept his little sister from falling down the steps, and yet again when he offered his brother a turn on his bicycle.

And now the boy's parents were happy. His father said, "The sunshine that helped the oak tree grow has found its way into our son to help him become a blessing to this house."

This was the grandmother's story. At least one of her grandchildren always remembered it.

The Stag, the Lion and the Eagle

A young prince once had a wicked stepmother who wanted her own son to inherit the kingdom. She employed a huntsman to take the prince out into the forest with orders to slay him. The huntsman, however, did not want to kill the boy himself, so he took him to the wildest part of the forest and left him there for the wild animals to devour.

The young prince knew no fear. He ate berries and nuts and drank from the brooks and streams. He slept beneath the sheltering trees and wandered through the wilderness, filled with wonder and love at the sight of nesting birds and growling beasts. So quietly and gently did he live and move that the wild things did not run from him but let him come among them as he wished.

One day, he found a stag whose antlers were caught in the branches of a tree and so could not lower its head to eat. The prince went up to the stag and loosened its antlers from the branches; the stag was then free to go on its way. But as the prince turned to go, the stag followed him and would not leave his side. It became his companion and journeyed with him wherever he wished to go, and the stag was often happy to carry the prince on his back.

Another day, the forest resounded with a loud roaring, and the prince and the stag searched until they found a lion caught in a hunter's net. Fearlessly, the prince approached the unhappy beast and loosened the ropes that bound it. Now the lion was free. It could have leaped upon the stag and the boy and devoured them with its mighty jaws, but instead it tenderly licked the hand of the child who had freed it. As the prince and the stag moved on, the lion followed them and became their companion.

Not long after that, the three companions came upon a wounded eagle lying in pain at the foot of a high cliff. Its wing was pierced through with a hunter's arrow. The prince approached the great bird, pulled the arrow from its wing, and stroked its head. While the eagle was recovering from its wound and was unable to fly, the prince brought it food and drink. At last its wound was healed, and it flew high into the sky. But as the prince, the stag, and the lion journeyed on, the eagle followed them and became their companion.

So it was that these four dwelt together as friends. The stag would carry the prince when he was tired. The lion would guard him as he slept. The eagle would fly overhead, keeping watch and guiding them away from dangerous places.

The prince lived with his three faithful friends for many a day until he was a young man, and from each of his friends he learned a lesson of life. From the stag, he learned surefootedness on the most dangerous ground, for the stag could carry him along narrow ledges of rock on the faces of steep cliffs. From the lion he learned courage, for the lion guarded the prince's life with his own. From the eagle he learned watchfulness, for the eagle, flying high, could observe all that lay below.

Now that the prince was a young man, he thought of his father's kingdom, and a great desire to return filled his heart. His companions saw that every day he became more and more solemn and sad. As he and they had learned to speak with one another, they asked him why he was not happy. He told them that the time had come for him to return to his father's palace and to live once more among other human beings. The three beasts loved their prince dearly and did not want him to leave them, yet they wanted him to be happy.

"I will guide you to your father's kingdom," said the eagle, "but the arrow that you drew from my wing will find me again."

"I will carry you to the palace gates," said the stag, "but then I will be caught as before in the branches of a tree, and the soldiers of the king will kill me for venison."

"I will guard you against those who might try to keep you from your kingdom," said the lion, "but the hunters who trapped me before will capture me again."

And it happened just as the beasts had foretold.

Circling over the King's palace, the eagle marked the way home for the young prince. And as he did so, a hunter drew his bow, and the arrow pierced the eagle's heart.

The Prince rode up to the palace gate on the back of the stag and then dismounted to enter on foot. The palace guards and their dogs gave chase to the stag and drove it back to the forest where its antlers became hooked in the branches of a tree. It could not escape death at the hands of the soldiers.

As the lion roared and sprang at the guards so that the prince could enter the palace gate, the hunters threw a net over the lion and slew it with their spears.

In the meantime, the old King, hearing all the commotion at the palace gates, came forth and recognized his son, whom he had long thought dead. He embraced him and led him into the palace. The wicked queen had long since died, poisoned by her own sins, and the young Prince was given the kingdom by his father.

It is not easy to be a king who rules wisely and well, but a strange thing happened. Although the stag, the lion, and the eagle had all died, they were still so near and dear to the prince that they had become a part of him. As king, when he needed to be watchful, he would feel the eagle soaring near his head. When he needed courage, he would feel the great heart of the lion pulsing close to his own. And when he had to be sure-footed to make his way through danger, he could sense the strong and delicate limbs of the stag carrying him on his way without faltering or stumbling.

So he became a great king because he was as far-sighted as the eagle, as brave as the lion, and as steady as the stag.

The Four Brothers

Once upon a time, there was a great and wise King who ruled over a vast kingdom, and in the course of time he had four sons.

When the day came for the four brothers to leave their father's house and to go in search of kingdoms of their own, they said to the King, "O Father, thou art wise and mighty, ruler of a vast kingdom. We who now go forth in search of kingdoms of our own can but further and extend thy kingdom. Tell us the secret of your greatness that we may rule wisely and well and be true sons of our father."

Then said the King, "My sons, even as there are four of you, so do I rule my kingdom by the power of four thoughts, and in these four thoughts do I hold sway. In telling them to you do I make you a gift of my wisdom. If these thoughts become your deeds, then your kingdoms will prosper. The choice is yours."

The four brothers remained silent and listened as the King revealed the four most secret thoughts of his mind. Said the King:

> Four thoughts dwell in my mind;
> With them my kingdom bind.
> The first one is thus sure
> That all life must endure.
> The second one I know
> Is that all life must grow.
> The third is yet more real
> That all of life must feel.
> The fourth is ever so
> That all of life must know.
> To endure, to grow,
> To feel, to know,
> These thoughts dwell in my mind,
> With them my kingdom bind."

The four brothers then went forth from their father's house, taking with them this gift of wisdom in the words: "to endure, to grow, to feel, to know," and each brother tried to understand their meaning.

At first the four brothers traveled together. They journeyed far from their father's house down a path that had no turning. At length, they reached a place where the road divided into four branches. If there had been only two forks in the road, or five or six, they would have wondered which to take. But as there were just four, they plainly saw that they were to part, each one to go his own way.

"Remember the words of our father," they said to each other, "and let his wisdom guide us, that his thoughts may become our deeds, and that in the kingdoms we find to rule his kingdom will be extended." Thereupon they touched each other for the last time, and each one went his way along one of the four forks of the road.

Now we must remember that the four thoughts of the King had dwelt together in his mind just like four petals of a single flower. So too, as long as the brothers had traveled together down a single path, these four thoughts had been as one. But now that the four brothers had parted, each one began to wonder which of the four sayings was the best and which one to choose for himself.

One brother, who had turned toward the north, said to himself, "What could be better than for all things to endure and to last forever? That is my choice: My kingdom shall endure and last forever. I will make everything so solid and firm that nothing can destroy it."

The second brother said, as he went toward the south, "What could be better than for all things to grow? That would mean that they are alive. This is my choice: In my kingdom, all things will be alive, ever-growing, ever-changing, and always renewed."

As he traveled toward the east, the third brother thought, "What could be better than for all things to feel, to love the good and to hate the bad? This is my choice: that all beings in my kingdom will love what is good for them and hate what is bad for them."

Traveling toward the west, the fourth brother did not think as his brothers did. He did not wonder which of his father's thoughts was the best. Rather, he wondered which one would explain the meaning of all the others. He said to himself, "If I, and all who live in my kingdom, could but know the meaning of all my father's thoughts, then would his wisdom truly guide us. It must be that, of the four, to know is the key to such wisdom. This is my choice."

Thus it was that the four sons of the King established four kingdoms on earth, and the King's thoughts became their deeds.

He who chose the thought "to endure" built his kingdom with rocks and firm earth. His was the kingdom of wide plains and rolling hills, rocky cliffs and mountain peaks—the kingdom of earth itself!

He who chose the thought "to grow" filled his kingdom with growing life—grass, flowers, and trees that sent their roots into the kingdom of the earth, their shoots upward toward the Sun. The plants themselves were the second son's kingdom, forever growing, blooming, fading, letting their seeds fall to earth only to grow again.

The brother who chose the thought "to feel" peopled his kingdom with creatures who were not only alive but who felt hunger and moved busily over the earth in search of food, who felt love and took care of their young, who felt hate for all that endangered their lives and who fought for their food and for their loved ones. These were the animals, and it was their kingdom over which the third brother ruled.

In the kingdom of the fourth brother, who had chosen the thought "to know," lived beings who not only had a share in the other three kingdoms but also had a fourth power. They not only had firm bodies, growing bodies, and feelings of love and hunger and hate, but they also had the power to know and understand the earth, the plants, and the animals.

And so it was that, when the great and wise King learned how his four sons had extended his kingdom over the earth by transforming his thoughts into their deeds, he summoned them into his presence and spoke these verses:

>Four deeds on earth can well be found:
>To endure, to grow, To feel, to know.
>We meet all four the whole world round.
>
>The rocks of earth endure and bear
>The weight of foot, The grip of root,
>The wash of waves and windy air.
>
>The plants in earth do grow and wane
>As seed and flower Helped by the bower
>Of shining sun and splashing rain.
>
>The beasts on earth feel love or hate,
>With fang and paw Or beak and claw
>Each kind will fight for food and mate.
>
>And man can know the world's true need
>For rock and tree And beast, and he
>Can learn to do the four-fold deed.

The Story of a Child

There is a certain kingdom where none but children live. No grownups ever set foot in this beautiful land, for all grownups had left it long ago by a strange and dangerous path so full of twists and turns that they can never find their way back. This is the story of a child who, once upon a time, lived in that kingdom.

The children were very happy in their kingdom. They felt not the slightest fear, although outside the walls and beyond the hills that circled the green meadows and blue waters of their home flitted many cloudy, gray shapes that made a ceaseless effort to force their way over the high walls and capture the children.

The children played joyfully all day long in the flowering fields among the friendly creatures who were young, too, like the children—kittens and fawns, puppies and lambs, ducklings and baby chicks. At night, the children would close their eyes and smile in their sleep as if they enjoyed that too. There is no doubt that this was the happiest land in all the world.

Who ruled this kingdom and watched over it? On a pleasant hill in the midst of the meadows there stood a palace. The gray hosts beyond the hills could see it there, but the children did not notice it, for it was built of light, not of rock or wood, and the children thought it was part of the sunlight. In this palace lived one who was not the ruler but the guardian of the kingdom. He wore a cloak of sky blue silk and looked just like a part of the sky, so the children did not see him. Yet he constantly hovered near them.

He had many helpers who, in their fleecy white robes, looked like the summer clouds, so the children did not see them either, although every child was under the watchful care of one of the guardian's helpers. The helpers did their work at night while the children slept. It was a wonderfully important work!

At night, when the palace walls had darkened, a light still glowed from within it like a bright star resting just above the hill. This light shone out from a large star-shaped chest filled with shining jewels. But the jewels were not made of stone. Like the palace walls, they were made of light and each one was shaped like a star. This treasure was all for the children, and yet they never saw it. At night, while they slept, the helpers would work, carrying the little stars of light from the treasure chest to the sleeping children. Each helper would bathe his child from the top of his head to the tips of his toes with the light and take special care to brighten the child's eyes.

The children would smile in their sleep as the light soaked into them. For this is what it did! And in the morning when they opened their eyes, sure enough, they were full of light. Beams of light would flash from child to child as they looked toward each other. It was as if a star shone out from every child's heart, filling their eyes with light. And wherever they looked, they saw only what was beautiful and good. So they were full of joy.

One day, one of these children, so full of life and joy, set out alone to explore the land. He walked and skipped and ran along, singing and whistling and talking to himself.

Now the gray shapes flitting around beyond the walls of the children's kingdom, are not exactly enemies, but just the same, they have it in mind to try to capture a child for themselves. They saw the boy wandering about alone, and they began to leap and flutter and make an extra effort to get over those high walls. Among the tiniest of them was one who flapped his gray veils like wings and caught the breeze just right so that he soared over the wall quite suddenly and landed upside down in the green meadow. Quickly he righted himself and looked for the nearest shadow where he could hide his grayness, for he didn't want to be discovered by the light beings who were always watching over their children.

In the meantime, the little boy had traveled far and was tired. He lay down and rested under the shady boughs of a tree and, still humming and whistling to himself, he stared up at the summer clouds in the blue sky. He felt drowsy. He half-closed his eyes, and a shadow flitted in front of them. It was a tiny shadow. In the middle of it, two dark little eyes seemed to be peering into his. He was surprised and said, '"Hello! Who are you?"

Then a whisper answered, "Take me into your heart and you'll find out."

The boy had never closed his heart against anyone or any thing, so he didn't now, and the little gray shape was soon inside of him, talking to him in a whisper. The whispers were all questions. Instead of explaining who he was, the little shape kept asking questions: "Who looks after you? Aren't you afraid? Wouldn't you like to let me show you the world?"

No one had asked the child such questions before, so he just listened, wondering what they meant. Soon the whisperer stopped asking questions and started giving orders: "Go where I lead you, and you will learn many things. Look around at what I show you, and you will see things you've never seen before."

The little boy opened his eyes wide. Something had happened to them. The starlight in them was not as bright, for two dark little holes cast tiny shadows in the midst of the light. The little gray whisperer was looking out through the boy's eyes, and sure enough, the boy could see something he had never seen before—a beautiful palace on a pleasant hill. "Who lives there?" he cried.

"Why don't you go and see?" came the whisper.

He set off at once, and as he went toward the palace, the sky grew dark. The sun was setting. The boy should have gone home to bed, but he didn't think of that, so eager was he to reach the beautiful palace.

By the time he reached the palace gates, it was night. He saw many people dressed in flowing robes hurrying in and out through the gates. The whisperer in his heart guided him so that he could slip in unnoticed, among the people. He followed them into a great and splendid hall where a noble king, cloaked in blue silk, sat on a high, golden throne. At his feet lay a chest full of treasure—shining jewels as bright as stars. One after another, the King called the people to his throne and gave them a share of the treasure. The people hurried out with their treasure and came back for more.

"Don't let anyone see you," said the whisperer. "They might send you home to bed. Just stay with me in the shadows. You'll be able to watch everything."

The child did as he was told. He feasted his eyes on the jewels and longed to have some for himself. While he was watching from the shadows, one of the white-robed people came into the hall as if he were looking for someone who was lost. He looked here and there until his great, clear eyes fell on the boy in the shadows. Swiftly he came toward him and looked searchingly into the boy's eyes. The little gray companion hid itself in the darkest corner of the boy's heart, and all that the white-robed man saw was a very sleepy, little boy. Without a word, the man lifted the child in his arms and hurried him home to bed.

As soon as the child was asleep, the man rejoined his companions, gathering the treasure of light from the star-shaped chest in the guardian's palace and hastening to bathe the child with it as he slept. But it was nearly dawn and there was not much time left. Because of this, less light than usual soaked into the boy, and the small amount that did get into his heart was swallowed up by the little gray shape who was hiding there.

The next morning when the boy awoke, his eyes were not as shining as those of his friends. When he went out to play in the meadows, he barely looked at the flowers, and he hardly noticed the beautiful, blue sky where the white summer clouds were drifting. While all the other children were joyfully running and playing, the boy stood apart. Inside his heart he heard a whisper, "Remember the beautiful palace and the treasure you saw last night? It is still there, and I can guide you back to it.

"Come on!" the other children called to him. "Come and see the nest we have found. It holds five little eggs as blue as the sky."

"A nest holds only eggs!" whispered the voice. "That's nothing compared with a palace that holds treasure."

The boy looked toward the most pleasant hill in the kingdom. Sure enough, he could see the palace walls. He called to the other children, "Look! There is a palace on that hill. A king lives there. He has a chest full of jewels that he shares with the people. I have been there and seen him."

The children looked but could see no palace. They listened to what the boy was telling them as to a fairy story, and when it was over, they ran off to look at the blue eggs in the little nest.

You know more than they do," said the whisperer, "but they don't believe you."

"I'll make them believe me," answered the boy. He called on his friends to follow him to the palace. Some of them started out with him as he set off, but somewhere along the way, one by one, each child lost interest and turned back. Why go and look for something that isn't there? They would rather play with their fawns and kittens in the meadow with their friends.

"Never mind them," said the whisperer. "You know more than they do. If you go to the palace alone, you may be able to get some of the treasure for yourself."

When the boy reached the palace, he found the doors wide open. No one appeared to stop him, so he walked right in. Everything was as he remembered it. He went into the great hall. It was quite dark and cold. No one was there. The throne was empty and gray in color. The treasure chest was there before it. It had the shape of a star, but it was not shining. The boy tiptoed up to it. Inside his heart, the whisperer was leading him. Every whisper that he heard made him feel bolder. "Open the chest," whispered the voice inside him.

He reached out and touched the cover. As he did so, the little gray shadow in his heart began to leap and grow, just as the smoke from a candle flame grows when the light begins to sink. "Open the chest!" The whispering grew louder and sounded like a wild wind in the treetops.

The boy did as he was told and looked into the chest. There lay the treasure, star-shaped jewels now dim and dark as if the gray shadow had leaped right out of the boy's eyes and darkened their brightness.

"Take some for yourself," whispered the voice, with a sound of rushing water. The boy quickly filled his pockets.

When the boy left the palace with his pockets full of jewels, the gray shape was no longer such a tiny thing hiding in his heart. It had stretched out and grown into his hands and feet, just as if the boy's own shadow were inside of him instead of outside on the ground. His hands and feet felt heavier and heavier with the dark shadow stretching out into them. He could hardly lift his feet, let alone run and skip with the other children.

When, at length, he got back to the meadow, he found the children in a circle. They were very quiet. Their eyes were shining. They had their ears turned toward a leafy bush as if listening for a sound. As the boy joined them, one of his friends pointed toward the bush and said very softly, "We can hear the baby birds inside the eggs pecking at the shells, wanting to be born."

"That's nothing!" said the boy. "I have been to the king's palace." The other children looked at him strangely for they did not understand what he meant. "There is a great treasure in the palace," said the boy. The children still stared at him, not knowing what he meant. "Shining jewels, like stars," the boy went on. "I have seen them."

"He's just pretending!" said one of the children.

"Listen!" exclaimed another, "the little birds! Let's stay here until they come out of the eggs."

The circle of children became quiet again. The boy looked at the children. They seemed to be far away from him, although he was right there with them. He felt as if he were all alone. They were with each other.

"Show them what you have," whispered the voice inside of him. Then the voice became so loud that it crackled and roared like a flame of fire. "Show them. Then they'll know what you mean!"

"I have some of the King's treasure myself!" cried the boy in a loud voice. "I can show it to you." The children turned to look. Their eyes were wide and shining with that starry light that showed them all that was beautiful and good in the world.

The boy reached into his pockets and filled his hands with what was there. He took the treasure out and held it in his hands for the others to see. Then he looked at their faces and waited to hear what they would say.

Looking at what he had in his hands, they saw a few lumps of mud, and they laughed. Looking at his face, they saw two great shadowy holes instead of his blue eyes, and they were frightened and ran away.

While the boy had been showing the stolen treasure, the gray shadow inside of him had raised itself up into his head and looked darkly out through his eyes. Now it began to stretch out all around him like a dark cloud. As it grew larger, it grew stronger, and the little boy had to go with it wherever it led him. Before he knew what was happening, the big, gray shape was carrying him off, away from the meadow and toward the circle of hills outside the walls of the kingdom. Then, in what seemed like one short moment, the boy found himself in the midst of all those gray, flitting shapes that surrounded the bright land of the children. Now he was captured.

He heard the voices of the gray shapes all around him. They sounded like winds, waves, and crackling flames, all telling him he was captured. "You are captured – captured –" they sighed and snapped. "Captured!"

In this new, gray land, there was no one for the boy to play with. He saw other captured people but they had forgotten how to play. They were all more grown up than he was, and he saw that they were all seeking and searching for something with worried eyes and hardly a smile. They seemed to have lost something important, and he did not understand what they said to each other. From the gray hills, he could look back into the sunny, beautiful kingdom he had left. He could see the children running joyfully in the meadows, and he wished he could get back to them. His pockets were still filled with the treasure he had taken for himself—little, dark lumps of mud that did not make him happy. And the gray shadow who had captured him never left him. The gray shadow loved to talk, but it didn't know how to play.

"Let me go back to the other children," begged the boy. "Show me the way back to them."

"The way is closed," answered the whisperer, "and the walls are higher than you think, for you have helped to build them up."

"I was so happy there," cried the boy.

And the gray shadow answered, "There were those who made you happy there. Now and forever after you will have to make your own happiness."

The boy began to weep. The tears flowed all through him like a river of sadness. And as the waters of the river of sadness washed through him, the gray shadow was washed out and floated away. Even the muddy treasure he had gathered was washed out of his pockets. At last the boy felt clean. Now he wept no more but dried his eyes and saw that he stood in a fair country. The sun was shining on a peaceful, green hill where a shepherd was watching over a flock of white sheep.

A Time of War

Two boys, who were cousins, grew up together in the years when the Huguenots were revolting against the Catholic Church in France. They were both sons of knights and, as children, they looked forward to becoming brave knights like their fathers. Happily they played together the kind of game in which they pretended to be fearless warriors, loving comrades loyal to each other unto death.

There were recurring wars in France, and the boys heard, on the one hand, the heartless talk of their fathers' companions—accounts of battles, plans for revenge, deeds of arms, and deaths of comrades—and on the other hand, the fears of their mothers and sisters. Louis enjoyed the talk of the men with a strange kind of fascination and did not pay much attention to the women's talk, while Pierre was much more aware of what the women said. Their worry and their grief affected him deeply.

This difference in their natures became more striking as they grew older, and their happy way of playing together began to change. More and more, Louis enjoyed the chance to be rough and warlike, while Pierre became more thoughtful and could always see the dead after the game of war was over. They began not to understand each other.

Each boy had a guardian angel, and though neither boy knew it, their angels always hovered near them. It was the task of the angels to see that Louis and Pierre remained together in life until they had learned something from each other.

At the same time, equally unknown to either boy, two dark spirits came to make use of them. Like the angels, these demons had a task, and that was to create misunderstanding between the two cousins. Demons like to find homes in the souls of human beings. They can undo much more in the world through human beings than by themselves. The demon who set himself up in the soul of Louis took his seat in Louis' head. There he made himself into a small speck of darkness but was able to lengthen out like a long, dark tongue—sharp as a blade of steel—and he could take possession of Louis' tongue and make Louis say things that were willed by the demon. The other demon, who moved into the soul of Pierre, was like a cloud that spread itself all around him just under his skin, covering Pierre's soul with a web of darkness through which the boy could not go out to mingle with other people. Nor could those who loved him find their way to his heart.

Pierre became the prisoner of his demon, while Louis became the weapon of the dark spirit in him. As the two boys grew to be young men, they were no longer happy together. Louis often spoke sharp, cutting words as if to wound his cousin. Pierre withdrew his friendship more and more with an unhappy feeling of helplessness. Louis took more and more interest in the events of the times, while Pierre found it hard to feel any interest in them.

The wars in France had become civil wars. Brothers and neighbors were fighting each other, some as Huguenots, others as Catholics. Louis' sympathies were with the Huguenots. To him they represented the spirit of freedom. He was irritated that Pierre did not share his sympathies. Pierre seemed to be living in a world of his own, which Louis could not enter. In time, Louis lost all love for his cousin, all sense of companionship, and at last one day, he spoke some fatal words.

"You," said Louis to Pierre, "haven't the spirit of a man or a knight. Everyone sees that. How you quiver and squirm inside your skin like a frightened animal, cornered and at bay! I loathe you near me, and when you come into the great hall, the fellows wish you were elsewhere!"

Hearing each word, Pierre was in great misery. Louis turned his back on him and left the place. This was their last moment together. Louis had pierced his cousin as if with a sword. It meant nothing to Louis anymore, but Pierre felt the pain of the wound.

The next morning in the bright sunshine, Louis rode away to offer his services to one of the Huguenot leaders. But already before dawn, Pierre had started off on foot to the nearest monastery where, as a monk, he would try to find healing for his wound.

The two angels of Louis and Pierre now became greatly enlarged in size, and as the two cousins increased the distance between each other, their two great angels reached across the distance to touch each other's hands.

The violence of the fighting between the Huguenots and the Catholics increased and spread. Each side was as ruthless and bloody as the other. The Huguenots attacked churches and monasteries. Louis took part in the bitterest events. One night, in an attack on a monastery in the neighborhood of his uncle's manor, Louis killed

Pierre, not knowing whom he had slain. As he went forward with the Huguenot band before dawn toward a new objective, the death of Pierre meant nothing to him. The Huguenot raiders, in turn, were surrounded shortly after dawn by an army of the Catholic Duke of Guise, and in the encounter Louis lost his life.

The souls of Pierre and Louis now dwelt in purgatory where there was no day or night, no change of season, no passing of time. There was only a sense of failure in which every soul came face to face with those people and events it had failed to understand in life on earth. Here each soul felt the pain, which in life, it had inflicted on others.

Louis did not understand his fate in purgatory. Around him were many souls. He thought he recognized among them some of his comrades who had died in battle. But whenever he tried to draw near them, a sword barred the way. The sword was pointed toward him. It was a long, dark sword that flickered like a sharp tongue, and it uttered biting and painful words that cut into him and gave him great pain. This he had to endure.

Pierre, likewise, did not understand his fate. He felt himself to be homeless and longed to find some place, among all the throngs of souls, where he could lie down or sit or lean. But whenever he seemed to find a seat or a bed or a post to lean on, someone else was already there, and this was always the same dark form. Pierre was forced to wander hither and thither among the hosts of souls in purgatory, unable to find a resting place.

Above, in the free space of heaven, the guardian angels of Louis and Pierre hovered, looking down upon their two charges in purgatory, waiting for the moment when the two souls could free themselves from that place. The angels waited and waited. They were patient and hopeful. They waited until Louis could hear exactly the wounding words that pierced him and gave him pain—until Pierre could see clearly the face of the dark form that always took the place he wanted.

Then Louis heard the words uttered by the sword-like tongue and realized that they were the last words he had allowed himself to speak to his cousin, Pierre. And Pierre saw that the dark form was molded in his own likeness, in every detail of his earthly face and figure.

Now, both Louis and Pierre felt a great need to live again more wisely as men upon the earth. Together they rose up toward their angels whom they now saw clearly. In the shining eyes of the angels, there was understanding for the longing that united the hearts of the two cousins.

About the Author

Elizabeth Gardner Lombardi's Recollections of Dorothy Harrer

I was privileged to have Dorothy Harrer as a teacher for three years at the Rudolf Steiner School in New York City from fourth grade through sixth grade during the 1940s. She stood about 5 foot 2 inches, with short, curly hair which I remember as grey mixed with dark brown. Mrs. Harrer took many students through eight years as a class teacher, but this was her first class, and I was very aware or her working hard to prepare lessons. She had taught previously in a poor section of Appalachia, where one of her students confided in her about experiences with elementals. She herself had a genuine relationship with the spirit.

Brought up in India as a child, she made the myths and history of that country very alive for our class. This was also true of her sharing tales from the Iroquois. She had both a talent for the English language and a gift for drawing. She also had a talent for appreciating the gifts of each child, not only encouraging us, but also challenging us to expand our expectations. For each student she wrote a special verse and had us take turns reciting the verses before class in the morning. [Three of those verses are included in this collection.]

Dorothy and her husband William founded Camp Glen Brook, 250 acres of farmland and forests in the New Hampshire mountains where students from the City could experience the calming influence of nature without media. Camp included crafts, music, drama, sports and hikes. Dorothy's special domain was the care of the animals. Sunday mornings the entire camp would convene for singing and an inspiring story.

The Harrers bequeathed this property to the Waldorf School of Garden City, NY, whose students and adults visit often, working side by side to tend the farm animals, maintain buildings and grounds and complete whatever chores this rural setting requires, where children come to appreciate their own imaginations, the company of others, and wonder of the natural world.

In the years I knew the Harrers, there were no teacher training centers in the US, and teachers helped each other and studied what had been written for the first Waldorf School teachers in Stuttgart, Germany. One could say that Dorothy Harrer was one of the pioneer class teachers – sturdy, a real doer. Responsible for much of the early literature published in English about the Waldorf curriculum, her books are still widely used in Waldorf schools in English-speaking countries.

Mrs. Lombardi herself had no formal training when she became a Waldorf teacher a year after graduating from Oberlin College, OH, though by that time there were three schools in the US following Steiner's pedagogical indications.

Made in the USA
San Bernardino, CA
06 December 2014